Prowler!

The wind coming from the north was gentle on my back. It felt wonderful, but from where I stood, it put my scenting instinct at a disadvantage. Suddenly I felt a tug at my paw. General Henry was trying to kick me in the shins, which was about as high as he could get.

I had a tremendous urge to step on the little creep. I mean, enough was enough.

But the general wasn't playing games.

His eyes were frantic. He was running around in circles trying to get my undivided attention without barking.

When I turned to follow him, the wind told me what it had already told him.

Someone was trespassing. . . .

JUDGE BENJAMIN: SUPERDOG

Judith Whitelock McInerney

Drawings by Leslie Morrill

AN ARCHWAY PAPERBACK
Published by POCKET BOOKS • NEW YORK

An Archway Paperback published by
POCKET BOOKS, a division of Simon & Schuster, Inc.
1230 Avenue of the Americas, New York, N.Y. 10020

Text copyright © 1982 by Judith Whitelock McInerney
Illustrations copyright © 1982 by Leslie Morrill

Published by arrangement with Holiday House Inc.
Library of Congress Catalog Card Number: 81-85092

ISBN: 0-671-46291-1

First Archway Paperback printing December, 1983

10 9 8 7 6 5 4 3 2 1

Printed in the U.S.A.

IL 4+

For J.B.

Chapter 1

Decatur, Illinois isn't exactly the Swiss Alps, but I guess it doesn't need to be. A St. Bernard can find happiness in middle America as long as he is with the people he loves.

That's me. Judge Benjamin.

The big bloke of a pet, who, instead of snowy rescues, uses his talents (and I use the term loosely) to make one family safe and secure.

Nine years ago the O'Rileys found me at the bottom of a pile of ten sisters. They could not afford me and bought me on time payments—can you believe that? There were just three of them then, Mr. and Mrs. O'Riley and that chunk of a child Seth. The O'Rileys had barely enough room in the small rented house even

1

without me, but we managed. We had a weeping willow out in front and a tiny square of grass that made a patch of backyard just big enough for a picnic.

Seth and I chewed shoes together in the teething stages, shared Popsicles in the playful stages, and welcomed the sister that came soon after.

Little Kathleen opened up a whole new ball game. She was pretty and lively and as soon as she could talk, could she ever!

Ann Elizabeth was the next surprise. And speaking of surprises, she had all the sweetness of a Marine sergeant when it came to getting what she wanted. Or else she managed to be the perfect little lady. You could never let your guard down, because she got you either way.

There were job transfers for Tom O'Riley, and bigger houses, and one day we landed in Decatur. It was a good fit, I guess, because Tom decided to set down roots. Tom opened his own construction glass business and bought the house where we live now.

Ten-year-old Seth, eight-year-old Kathleen, and three-year-old Ann Elizabeth weren't babies anymore—they were slimming down and growing up and becoming quite independent. Now Maggie O'Riley was expecting again, just when I'd begun to relax. Come spring. Man may work from sun to sun, but a St. Bernard's work . . . well, you know. I had a twenty-four-hour job to do.

September had just slipped into October and the huge yard, though still decked in summer green, was cool and pleasant. A St. Bernard can enjoy the crisp evenings and cold firm ground like few humans. The thinning of my coat in summer makes room for the rich, thick insulation that, thank heaven, no women find fashionable.

I guess it needs a big square nose and two black eyes to give it class.

Maggie sent me out back with the kids on this wonderful Friday morning to clear the cushions off the patio furniture. The flurry of activity put a damper on my early morning ritual of being alone, but today I didn't mind. I knew there must be something in the wind since Maggie had been cleaning all week.

Ann Elizabeth climbed up to the second branch of the Jonathan dwarf apple tree to supervise. Seth and Kathleen must have thought this was a good idea because they didn't complain.

Seth was getting big. He had unzipped his parka and was stretching to reach the swing canopy. He grimaced, but he got it. A smile of triumph crossed his freckled face.

Kathleen paused when she spotted the remains of a spider on the swivel cushion. Tossing her black braids, she called to Annie to dispose of the "pretty bug," and went on with her work.

"Mom surely has been knocking out the chores this week. It's not even seven o'clock, it's barely light, and we haven't had breakfast. My stomach's really growling," she said.

Now she was talking my language. I'd been up for two hours, and I hadn't had so much as a doughnut. That wasn't like Maggie. I'd had to put up quite a fuss just to get my bowl of milk. The family breakfast was a tradition. Maggie and Tom had decided long ago that it was important to have some special time together. Mornings were the best opportunity.

Seth was piling the last of the cushions by the back door. "Ummm, I think it's going to be worth waiting for. Something smells awfully good."

I turned in the direction of the kitchen and took a good long sniff.

Seth was right. Canadian bacon, hash browns, some kind of egg casserole, and—oh, great—butterscotch rolls. On a weekday? Something was definitely up.

The rumbling in my stomach was deafening.

After an eternity of three more minutes, Maggie called us in.

Ann Elizabeth looked like she had fallen into

a mulch pile. I expected Maggie to scold her—Maggie had dressed her in those clean clothes only twenty minutes before—but when we marched in Maggie was humming and smiling.

I smelled a bribe.

I also smelled the breakfast goodies first-hand.

We all sat down and Tom led the customary grace.

Five individual thank yous followed. Maybe one of the reasons I like our home so much is because all appreciate the simple things.

The breakfast was a pleasure. Maggie had saved me the bacon trimmings. I took my post under the table to wait for more dividends. Even Tom was generous with the tidbits. Usually, he lectures about not feeding a dog from the table.

The butterscotch rolls were fantastic—yeast dough with pudding, brown sugar–pecan–coconut filling, and the caramelized glaze!

Yum. It was a great way to start my day. Little did I know that from that point on the day would proceed downhill with all the speed of a rolling stone.

"Guess who's coming for a visit?" Tom asked.

He got two rounds of answers, all wrong, before he decided to let us know. "Grammy and Henry."

I don't know whether it was a bit of hash browns or a bit of coconut that caught in my throat, but it was a foreboding for sure. Everyone else was cheering so hard that they didn't even notice my choking. I managed to regain my composure as Tom went on.

"They'll be here tonight."

I knew they were talking about Maggie's mom when the name Grammy came up, but Henry? At first I thought Grammy had given Pa, Maggie's father, the boot and this was a new friend. But in this family the people who get married stay married, so I dismissed the idea.

Henry . . . Henry . . . now where had I heard that name before?

A very large lump began to form in the pit of my stomach as it came to me. Henry was Grammy's dachshund, and if ever there were tales of a dog that was unmanageable!

But wait, they were still talking.

Maggie was excited.

"This is going to be a very special visit. It will just be you kids and the Judge and Grammy and Henry. Daddy and I are going to combine a little business and pleasure and fly up to Green Bay, Wisconsin for a few days."

I was in shock.

What did they mean, taking off and leaving me in charge of three children, a Grammy, and a delinquent dachshund? All right, I was here to love, honor, and protect my family, but this was asking a heck of a lot. Three days? Four? It might as well have been a month.

Seth was in his glory. "You mean I can take care of myself? Do I get to stay up late? What about desserts?"

Well, at least there was a man after my own heart.

"Grammy will be making those decisions starting tomorrow morning. She's pretty strict on bedtimes, but she's an ole softie when it comes to desserts."

My mind began to wander to the first time Grammy had laid eyes on me. All she could say was that anyone who kept a pet bigger than a bread box was crazy. But Maggie's tears prompted a change of heart. The next day Grammy brought a peace offering, a warm scrumptious pecan pie. And she cut a special piece for me.

Kathleen's wheels were turning too. "If Grammy sleeps in the guest room downstairs, she won't be able to hear Annie, so I'll have to handle her. Grammy's probably forgotten about little kids and stuff. It's been a long time since you were little, Mom."

Ah, Kathleen, what I could tell you about tact!

Maggie's mood was so good she went right

8

on. "It would be wonderful if you would, Kathleen. There is a lot Grammy will need help with. Sometimes the three of you are more than I can handle, so whatever you can do to help will make it that much easier for her."

I could see this was not a matter to be voted on, but was in the final stages of "activate," and I was powerless to protest. When had Maggie and Tom talked about it? I prided myself on knowing all that went on in this house. It must have been during one of their pillow talks, that time that married people have together when even Santa Claus and the Easter Bunny aren't welcome. Before you know it, the commitments are set and you are quarterbacking a big game plan.

"Pa will be bringing Grammy and Henry to Sandoval, where I'll meet them," said Tom.

"Are they going to fly there?" Kathleen broke in.

"No, Grammy is afraid Henry might get airsick."

Oh, brother. He was shaping up as more of a ding-a-ling every time they mentioned him.

Tom went on, "They'll be here in time for a late supper tonight. Then tomorrow, very early, Maggie and I will take off for the airport."

It was Seth's turn. "Who's going to be the pilot in command, Dad—you or Mom?"

Maggie was laughing. "It was a struggle, but Dad agreed to let me fly up, and he'll fly back. I think it's so I'll have to do the hardest navigating—he'll just have to reverse my plan, with minor wind correction."

Tom pretended to be hurt. "Why, Maggie, you know how sincere I am about equal rights!"

Annie Elizabeth said very quietly, "I didn't get any rice. Is there equal rice for me?"

Kathleen chuckled and almost spat out her hot chocolate.

Everyone was laughing and having a good time.

Except me.

My mind kept zeroing in on the havoc the next days could mean.

My kingdom was going to be subdivided.

Chapter 2

All that day I got into trouble. I managed to be in the wrong place at the wrong time, and Maggie, always a bit fussy before company, was laying it on me pretty hard.

When Tom left for work and Seth and Kathleen hopped the bus for school, I began my descent into the pits.

Maggie asked me to keep an eye on Annie while she made out payrolls for Tom. It was my favorite job, really. I just had to block the electrical outlets and other hazards when Annie Elizabeth got a dangerous notion to experiment.

I didn't have my mind on my work though. I kept thinking about Henry being underfoot. Being an only dog was all I had ever known.

Did this mean I'd have to share the leftovers? And just where was this clown going to sleep? I mean, all the good spots were taken—by me!

And another thing—Maggie wouldn't be around to insure my rightful position. After all, Henry was Grammy's dog, so I was suddenly going to b number two.

My basic lazy streak didn't relish the idea of trying harder.

For a while I could hear Annie carrying on a running conversation with Maggie. Annie chattered and Maggie ummhummed, somehow interpreting the tax charts and getting the checks right. Then silence. It lasted too long. I looked around and was surprised to see that Annie was no longer on the rug with me.

Well, she couldn't have strayed far. I'd only been daydreaming a minute. Or had I?

I looked behind the chairs, the couches, under the tables. Then I tried the bedrooms. No Annie. Maybe behind the curtains?

I was just pushing the drapes to one side, when I heard Maggie walk up behind me.

"Judge Benjamin! My white sheers!"

Annie came out of hiding to make a little echo right behind her.

"Judge! Mommie's zeers!"

Yup. They were right. There was a big black pawprint on the curtain and no one within a

12

hundred miles could claim a pawprint like that. Bigfoot was last seen in Canada.

Maggie had just laundered those drapes for Grammy's visit.

It would be hard to describe the hysteria in Maggie's usually lilting voice. But to a dog's sensitive ears, it was like a bomb going off directly behind my eyeballs. When I tried to cower to make myself scarce, my tail swept the top of Maggie's vanity. With an intensity much like Hurricane Hannah, the perfumes and creams in their delicate crystal bottles plunked and splattered every which way.

I don't know which was stinging more—my nose, which was assaulted by the colognes, or my pride, which was absolute shame when I saw Maggie's tears. Behind the bedlam stood little Annie, and behind her was a trail of something very wet and white.

Uh oh.

She had been in the bathroom cabinet and discovered the toilet paper. Someone had made the mistake of leaving the lid up on the toilet, and after stuffing a couple of rolls down the plumbing, she had wetted down another roll and driven it like a Grand Prix race car through the hall.

Why hadn't I heard Annie vrooom-vroooming?!

The friction had caused the wet matted paper to fall apart. Bits of it were ground into the shag carpet like sticky snowflakes.

Smoke was coming out of Maggie's ears and, since I was the babysitter in charge, it was meant for me.

As soon as I saw an opening I ran—out the back door and behind the forsythias. I felt guilty as sin, but I wasn't fool enough to stick around during the cleanup.

So there I was, ousted already, and Henry hadn't even arrived.

It was a funny, drab day. The sky was not as pretty as it had been the last couple of weeks. There were not even any interesting clouds to watch. The ceiling was high and a little gray, kind of the way I felt. It appeared to be a stationary front, and I figured it might hang around for a while.

After several hours of ignoring me, Annie's voice twinkled out the back door. "Judge Benjamin, where are you?"

She was carrying my lunch. Either Maggie was out of paper plates or she had decided I didn't deserve one, because my food was served on newspaper.

Dear Annie explained, "I sneaked this out, Judge. You're in big tubble."

So that was it. Annie, not Maggie, felt sorry for me.

Annie unfolded the paper. She had trouble as it kept sticking to the treasure inside.

"My favorite for you. Peanut butter and honey and cimmum and brown sugar. On raisin bread."

Now, I didn't want to sound ungrateful, but honey and cinnamon and brown sugar? That was a bit much. Not only that, but it was open faced, and my Friday horoscope by Jeane Dixon had to be peeled away from the top layer of honey.

It was tough to read through the goo:

Leo: On every side there are expressions of good will and indications of profitable combinations. Stir yourself to make the best of it.

I wondered if I should believe that. Maybe Henry's reputation was undeserved.

I wasn't giving him a chance.

I made the most of my mostly carbohydrate lunch and decided to follow Annie back into the house. She wadded up the newspaper and threw it in the garbage can on the way in. Then she stood on top of the can to secure the lid and divebombed feet first to the ground.

I was about to apologize to Maggie when I realized I'd walked in on another very sticky situation. There I stood, with evidence of honey and sugar matted in the hair on my ears, and there Maggie stood, surveying a counter that looked like it had been hit by an earthquake.

Annie, in spite of all her delightful qualities of independence, had hardly mastered neatness.

The peanut butter knife was stuck on the toaster. The honey jar was on its side, its contents spilling all over the stove. Sugar was in little mounds, up and down, everywhere, and Annie had attacked the remains of the loaf of bread on the floor, trying to dig out the raisins.

I made a U-turn and got out before the sparks flew.

Forget how good tomorrow is supposed to be, Jeane Dixon. . . . How am I supposed to get through today?

A low profile was the only solution.

My old standby was a long nap under the apple trees.

A few hours later, the school bus pulled up in front of our drive. I ran out to meet Seth and Kathleen. We played a quick game of tag (it pays an old dog to keep in shape), and then I faded into the house in the shadow of their schoolbooks.

Maggie noticed me sooner than I had hoped.

She ignored me at first, but that was better than another scolding. Then, in the soon forgiving manner that was hers, she handed Seth a brush and told him to groom me. On our way out back, she slipped me a handful of gingersnaps, a sure sign we were friends again.

Kathleen drilled Seth on his spelling words while he combed and curried.

I heard Tom's car in the driveway, and I knew it was the moment of truth.

Seth gave me one last swish with the brush and went racing to meet the car.

Kathleen stopped long enough to gather the schoolbooks and put them in place on the way.

My paws felt like they were in cement buckets. They just didn't want to move.

Then the giggling and squealing began, and my curiosity got the best of me. I walked around to the front of the house very quietly.

Chapter 3

There he was, sniffing the potentillas as if they were his.

Little flecks of gray streaked his shiny black hair. When he didn't take a deep breath, his long belly dragged across the high spots of the ground. He stood no higher than the callus on my right front foreleg, but he cocked his head like a Prussian general. I felt like a submarine about to be put under siege by a PT boat with a secret weapon. Instead of laughing at his arrogance, it made me uncomfortable, never mind that I could eat his weight in Gainesburgers and call it a light snack.

He made an unbecoming snarl that let me know he was as happy about this visit as I was.

To my surprise, Grammy scolded him immediately.

"Henry Von Girard! You're a guest and you'd better behave like one."

That label certainly sounded fit. The only thing missing was "general." Yes, now that really fit. General Henry Von Girard.

He stopped snarling but continued to sneer. It would be hard to say which was less gracious.

Grammy had hugs for all the kids and set to finding the orange chewies she'd brought as a treat.

Goodness, how I loved those.

Grammy was a gem, and I knew we would get along. She has the same kind of sparkle and no-nonsense discipline as Maggie. They are a lot alike inside, even though outwardly they are absolute opposites. Maggie is tall and plumpish. Grammy is a little bit of a thing. Her silver hair in its tight curls is nothing like Maggie's dark, simply combed style.

Grammy even had a big hug for me. Now, how could such a sweet Grammy have such a pickle of a canine?

General Henry and I got through the evening by playing musical rooms. We were never within twenty feet of each other.

He had a snort that would move mountains.

When I heard him coming down the hall, I would nap in the bathtub. When he picked the parlor sofa to pounce on, I hid under Maggie's bed. And when he lay, arrogantly and outrageously, in my spot to catch leftovers at the dinner table, I played the perfect host and pretended not to notice.

Maggie very tactfully fed us at different times. Grammy solved the sleeping situation by having Henry stay in the room with her.

It was strangely quiet on Saturday morning. Tom loaded the suitcases in the car. Maggie gave me a very special pat and whispered, "Take care of everything, Judge." Then they both kissed and hugged everyone and left. When the car was out of sight, it was two very long minutes before anyone moved.

Seth was chewing on his bottom lip. Grammy was pretending a speck got in her contact. Finally, Kathleen scooted Annie Elizabeth on her hip and said, "Got any more orange chewies, Grammy? I think the Judge could use some cheering up."

Me?! Oh, well, I'd been the scapegoat for worse.

General Henry nearly tripped me going up the front step, and his stiff, pointed black tail hit me right in the eye.

What a jerk.

I was beginning to feel this family wasn't big enough for both of us. But I remembered Maggie's last words.

Once inside, Grammy got the wonderful idea of Dairy Queen ice cream for everyone. The orange chewies had disappeared. There was a piece of plastic bag caught on Henry's paw, but I couldn't prove anything. Grammy loaded the kids in the Gremlin and promised to bring a treat back for us. Then, not sure how things were between Henry and me, she decided to leave us in the garage instead of the house.

Now, I had never been a garage animal and I didn't like it. I would have preferred the open spaces of the backyard, but the slightest bit of precipitation was spitting out of the sky and Henry shivered every time a drop hit his nose. Naturally, he would have melted, or so Grammy thought.

We could hear a commotion in the driveway—Grammy was having trouble getting the Gremlin in gear. A stick shift on the floor was not the same as the cruise-controlled, electric-seat-adjusted, automatic-light-group on her Cadillac back home. When she bucked the Gremlin a few feet, it sounded like a Great Dane barking and a cat shrieking alternately.

There was a pause and Seth came into the garage with Kathleen.

"Grammy decided you fellas better have this in case we're gone a while," Kathleen explained, setting down some Gainesburgers.

There were two bowls: General Henry's, a ceramic dish in crimson red with bold black letters spelling HENRY, and mine, an old five-quart saucepan Maggie had picked up for ten cents at a garage sale. Seth brought two more bowls, empty, and filled them with fresh water from the spigot in the corner of the garage. Seth didn't quite get the water turned off. I hoped the drip wouldn't give me a headache.

Kathleen took time for a quick pat on my head.

Then, once more, we heard the bucking and coughing of the Gremlin in Grammy's manicured hands.

Henry didn't even wait till they were out the garage door, let alone the driveway, before attacking his food.

I thought it was just a case of bad manners the way he wolfed down the one Gainesburger they had left for him, until I saw him stick his nose into my supply for more. I recognized it for what it was—a power play. With surprising speed, I got there just in time. Henry had deposited one of *my* burgers in his bowl. In the brief time it took him to take a breath, I slammed my paw down on his dish.

23

My moment of triumph was brief.

The startled look on Henry's face did my heart good, but it was accompanied by a crunching noise and a pain in the pad of my paw.

I had broken the sacred dish.

Henry was glaring at me and I was having second thoughts.

I tried to look apologetic, but Henry was planning his attack. He was no slouch in spite of his pipsqueak status. He moved like lightning up onto the wheelbarrow, his paw deliberately dislodging the rakes hanging from the wall.

I moved out from under them just in time.

Then he spotted a series of convenient steps—boxes, fertilizer bags, tools—that got him up on the stack of firewood and close enough to knock off Seth's Huffy bike hanging from its overhead rack.

He was a dog possessed, a general on blitzkrieg.

But the Huffy was a step too far.

The handlebars grazed my ear and banged my leg. As the bike landed, the kickstand caught on the faucet handle. When I pulled myself out from under the bike, the kickstand pulled too, and water began pouring out.

Henry saw it too, and we both panicked.

We had to find a way to stop it. The drain

was on the outside of the garage, and we were locked in!

Henry jumped off his perch, and we both studied the situation. If we could just push the kickstand back—but the bike was in the way. There was no way we could reach either the kickstand or the faucet.

I could think of only one good thing. Since the garage was situated under the house, the water wouldn't run into Maggie's clean floors inside.

Some comfort.

It didn't seem to take long before every square inch of the double garage was wet.

By the time the water rose to the top of my feet, it had also risen to the bottom of Henry's belly. He tried to get back on the wheelbarrow, but with his feet wet he kept slipping and finally knocked it over. He couldn't climb on top of the firewood either, because the boxes he had used as steps were now wet and collapsing.

It couldn't take long to get ice cream, could it?

But then there was a picture in my mind of Grammy stalled at every stoplight as she got the hang of Maggie's car.

I had no choice.

I got down on my knees so Henry could get on my back.

He didn't like the idea.

He gave me that snort that would buffalo a champion and stalked away.

The water kept rising.

I tried again.

Finally, his head bobbing stubbornly, he knew he couldn't last.

He got on my back the first try. He was so nervous that he hugged my neck more than necessary and the dog license around his neck got tangled in my choke collar.

If he had just held still, we would have been all right. But he panicked further. Pretty soon the chains of our collars were hopelessly linked. If I had had any sudden thoughts about changing my mind, it wouldn't have mattered. I couldn't let him drown without drowning myself.

Fate had made us allies.

We watched the water rise from a few inches to a foot. If Tom hadn't been so thorough in his insulation and caulking, more water might have leaked out. Instead, it began to cover the paint cans, the tool box, the golf clubs. Those sturdy garage doors were not budging.

Grammy, we both thought, wherefore art thou?

We could only guess.

I had a vision of a Brownie Delight, the hot

fudge dripping down the rich ice cream, the chewy brownies nesting in syrup. Seth was surely on the second banana of a tantalizing banana split with its warm sweet syrups. . . .

Meanwhile, we were swimming in cold dirty water, trying to avoid the floating firewood.

Chapter 4

When we finally heard the Gremlin sputter down the road toward home, I wondered how we could warn them. Would they notice the water barely leaking out under the door? Would they think it was wet from the early morning drizzle? I tried barking, but with Henry so firmly attached, it was hardly the old Judge warning system.

What if the water rushed out on little Annie?

I couldn't think of it.

I could hear the conversation in the driveway. "Seth, why don't you open the garage door for us?"

I tried desperately to bang my paw against the door to warn him.

Seth normally wasn't set on superspeed and that was our only salvation. He approached the door with his "Do I have to do my homework now," slow-foot shuffle, and very gradually pulled open the garage door.

He felt the rush of water on his feet at the same time he raised the door and stopped midway.

"Grammy, the door, close the car door!" Seth screamed.

Grammy was busy wiping the banana syrup off her blazer, so it was Kathleen who grabbed Annie back into the car, slamming the door with her other hand.

Just in time.

Seth swims. And the airtight Gremlin floats.

Within minutes the water was gone. Gone down the hill, into the drain, absorbed by the garden, just gone.

Henry and I ended up by the crabapple tree. The water was no longer surrounding us, but our collars were still firmly attached. Henry kept sliding down my side and I had to keep kneeling down to let him scramble back on top of me without choking both of us.

A very wet Seth was sitting in the driveway with a strange look on his face. I realized he must be thinking that he was the last one to turn off the faucet. He was probably blaming himself.

It just added to my guilt.

The car had been pushed only a few feet. The initial thrust of the water was over and the girls kept their heads.

Grammy got out to investigate and couldn't understand any of it. The garage was devastated. The only thing that hadn't been shuffled around was the Huffy bike. I was relieved when Seth saw that it was attached to the spigot. He knew then that the flood hadn't been his fault.

He looked at me and I hung my head. I'm sure he suspected that Henry and I had had some sort of fight, but he didn't let on.

Kathleen maneuvered Annie away from the muddy yard while Seth and Grammy went through the garage.

"This is most peculiar," Grammy commented. "It just makes no sense. How did the bike get there?"

Seth was looking at the general and me. "Oh, I guess they were just playing and it fell," he said finally. "You know how dogs roughhouse sometimes."

Grammy wasn't buying it. "Kathleen, come here and look at this. There has to be a specific explanation."

Kathleen jogged into the garage with Annie riding piggyback. "Whew! Those two did a number in here, didn't they?"

"But it doesn't make sense," Grammy persisted.

Seth was trying to give some kind of "cool it" signal to Kathleen, and she got the picture.

"Now you're talking, Grammy," Kathleen said, giggling. "Nothing about the Judge makes too much sense!"

Well, she didn't have to go that far.

But her strategy worked. Grammy was still puzzled, but she gave up asking questions.

Seth sighed deeply. In a rare moment of affection, he tugged Kathleen's braid and smiled lightly.

Kathleen was bringing the box of Dilly Bars up from the car (they were supposed to be a treat for two good dogs) when she noticed the arrangement of our collars. She tried to pull Henry and me apart, but the collars wouldn't budge.

Everyone tried.

Nothing.

Finally, Grammy decided things should be done in order: dry clothes for Seth, then Dilly Bars in the freezer for another day and, lastly, a drive to a locksmith to saw apart our collars.

The three children crowded into the sticky front seat, banana syrup and all, while Henry and I sat penitent and wet in the backseat. I am

the first to admit that wet fur is less than sweet-smelling.

Grammy opened the sun roof and Henry scooted to a perch on top of my head. He had fresh air and a view of the countryside.

Why do dogs like that always get the breaks?

Grammy stalled at so many stoplights that when she hit a green one she just kept going in second gear, at the monumental speed of fifteen miles per hour.

It must have been quite a sight. A man in a dairy truck did a double take, then slid off the road about ten feet.

Henry started barking at him, and that nearly choked us both.

Finally, we headed into the parking lot of Bob's Lock Shop.

It was full, naturally.

We had to find a place across the street at Walgreen's. Grammy decided to take the children into the store to purchase two new collars that she knew Henry and I would need after the collar cutting.

That left me to stare at the radio while Henry people-watched out the sunroof.

It was the lady with the white poodle's fault, or at least that's what Henry claimed later. He had to get a better look, he said.

There was a sudden tug at our connecting

collars and Henry started sliding down the front windshield, outside. Henry's black feet were dangling at my eye level.

Clumsy clod. My neck was going to be sore for a week after smacking into the rearview mirror as Henry's fall pulled me upwards.

I yanked him back into the car, but he didn't land on my head.

His bottom slapped the gear shift with a thud—into neutral.

I thought I had known panic before, but when the car started rolling, I was paralyzed with fear.

I could see Grammy running toward us.

I'm not completely sure whether what happened next was skill on the part of the general or just dumb luck. You can imagine the way he tells it. I do know that when we passed a row of plate glass windows I closed my eyes, certain the end was near.

But there was no great crash.

Henry kept pulling at my neck—I thought he was just slipping—but actually he was pawing at the wheel. Whatever, he managed to turn the car just enough so that the tires bumped the curb of a Fotomat island.

It was over that fast.

Except for Grammy's scolding. That seemed to last forever.

By the time we got in the lock shop, a crowd had begun to form, and a lot of fingers were shaking in our direction.

Henry was beginning to growl, and I suspected that anyone who got too close with a wagging finger would regret it.

A man's voice yelled, "You can't bring those unruly dogs into my clean shop!"

I figured that was Bob.

Henry's growl got louder and I started backing out. A key display met my left hip, but Seth caught it before it fell.

Grammy took control. "Then we'll require curb service."

Curb service? Was that a term from another generation?

Anyway, she steered us back outside.

We waited a few minutes but no one came out.

"I guess I didn't make myself clear," Grammy said. "We'll have to go back in."

"But what about the dogs?" Seth asked.

"They'll have to wait here," Grammy answered. She looked at us and said in her sternest voice, "Now, do you two think you can stay out of trouble for five minutes?"

We nodded.

They went back inside.

People walking by kept looking at us and laughing.

I wanted to hide—it was pretty embarrassing—but there weren't a lot of choice spots.

I saw a phone booth a few feet away and thought it might help a little. We huddled behind it.

As a hiding place, it definitely left something to be desired. A St. Bernard, wearing a black dachshund on his back, sitting behind a mostly glass phone booth. . . . Why, I couldn't have been more conspicuous if I had been *inside* wearing a bright red cape with a red S on it.

Superdog?

Well, I did have good intentions. . . .

I heard a roaring laugh and came back to reality.

Grammy was leading a sandy-haired man in scruffy blue jeans in our direction. One look at us and he was practically hysterical. "How . . . *how* did you do this?"

"Don't ask," Seth answered.

"Crazy! My gosh, these dogs must be dumb!" He just kept laughing.

I was not impressed.

Henry started growling again. Grammy held his mouth shut.

"Why don't you cut the collars?" Kathleen asked. "If my dad were home he would have it done in seconds."

Annie added her two cents. "But he's gonna be gone for days and days."

"Oh? I doubt that your dad would have the tools for this sort of thing anyway."

"He certainly would!" Seth said bragging. "My dad has all kinds of tools. Saws and belts and drills—he has a very important glass business."

The man stopped laughing long enough to hook up a long extension cord inside the shop. He had tried heavy wire-cutters first, but the collars were too tight to get the proper grip. He used a precision saw. I was nervous about a tool like that so close to my neck, and Henry started to howl with the loud, high-pitched whirring at his ears. But in a minute we were free.

The relief was instant. Grammy signed the receipt, paid the man, and we were on our way home.

To my surprise, General Henry didn't race away. In the car going home, he stretched out on the backseat right next to me.

It wasn't that we liked each other, but some measure of respect had begun to develop.

Grammy got the Gremlin into third gear.

Wow.

And she pulled into the driveway like a pro.

By four thirty Grammy had everything under control. She and the kids had laid out the tools and the firewood in the sunniest part of the yard to dry. Seth had cleaned the garage and replaced the dry tools. He left the garage doors open because the floor was still damp. Then we all headed for the kitchen so Grammy could build one of her famous feasts.

"C'mon, kids," Grammy said. "We've worked up a healthy appetite."

I couldn't argue with that.

Grammy made a yeast dough for rolls and assigned Annie to watch it rise. She had Seth grate cheese and Kathleen wash chicken parts.

Henry and I supervised.

"I think this was as busy a day as I've ever had," Grammy began, "but I think it would be best if we didn't tell Maggie and Tom everything till they come back. What do you think?"

"I think I'd like to see the look on Mom's face when she hears!" Seth said.

Annie dipped her finger in the dough but wasn't impressed with the taste. She directed a fingerful my way. Raw, unsweetened dough doesn't hold a candle to the finished product, and when Henry stepped in to make a grab for it, I let him have it.

He wasn't impressed either.

"You're right, Grammy," Kathleen said. "The less said the better."

"It won't be a fib. We just won't mention the crazy stuff," Seth offered.

39

Grammy looked relieved.

They made a pact over chicken in sour cream, cheese rice, spinach soufflé, and hot rolls. No one was to let on to Maggie and Tom that any great confusion had occurred.

"You see, kids," Grammy explained, "your mom and dad don't let me do much for them. But every so often, when they need to get away, they will ask me to help out. Maggie would stop doing that if she thought I couldn't handle it. And this is the best chance I have to get to know my grandchildren. So we'll just wait till they get back to tell all our adventures, okay?"

It was agreed.

When Maggie and Tom called at the expected time, Grammy gave glowing praises of how well-behaved the kids had been, and not one word passed her lips about delinquent dogs or a nearly grounded Gremlin.

While Grammy was still talking, Annie set off for parts unknown.

My instincts told me to follow.

She went directly to the extension in the bedroom.

My heart skipped a beat. She wouldn't!

She picked up the phone, listened for a minute, then volunteered, "We had a fud. And Henny and Judge Bejmin dove the car."

I heard Grammy drop the receiver in the

kitchen. Somehow, she managed to pick it up again and find her voice.

By the time the long distance call was over, Maggie and Tom weren't the only ones convinced we were managing quite well.

Grammy had us all believing it.

Chapter 5

Henry and I shared table scraps while Grammy read a story, said prayers, and tucked everyone in.

I was beginning to think our luck was changing.

That's when Grammy remembered that the garage doors were still open.

She went down in her nightgown to close them. I waited for the noisy rolling sound the doors always made. I heard the first one. Then, nothing.

More waiting.

Still nothing.

I went to make sure Grammy was all right and saw her doubled up.

"Judge. Hello. Now I've really gone and

done it. The water must have swelled the joists a bit. I gave the door more of a tug than I should have. I've thrown my back out."

By leaning on me, she made it into the house.

I was sure Grammy would call a doctor right then, but she said, "I was going to bed anyway." She struggled to the kitchen, fixed herself a little bourbon with a twist of lemon and a bunch of ice. Then she propped herself in bed with a complicated arrangement of pillows and books.

She fell asleep before the ice had melted.

Because Henry and I were not the cleanest dogs after our episode, we had to sleep out back.

Henry plunked himself on my spot by the back stoop. I called his bluff with my most assertive *"Woof!"*

He moved to the hearth of the outdoor fireplace. It put him slightly higher than my eye level lying down, which seemed to thrill him. He kept turning around and clearing his throat so I would be sure to notice.

I didn't mind so much. We'd been through a lot together in the last twenty-four hours. Henry's sneer had lost a little of its punch. In fact, I was almost to the point of no longer disliking him.

Until I realized he snored.

43

Not a little snore, mind you. A throat-warbling, sinus-joggling snore. And the weird thing about it was that it wasn't constant. No rhythm, no pattern, just every so often, it sounded like a truck backing into the patio.

I did my best to ignore it, but it was no use. Just when my eyes and bones would settle down, *"Hronksha!"* Henry would start snoring again.

So I went for a walk.

It was cool, a nice kind of autumn night.

I wandered past the apple trees and forsythias, out of range of Henry's snoring.

The earlier rain seemed to have cleaned the sky out. I could see the constellations plainly. I drew an imaginary line from the two stars at the end of the Big Dipper bowl to the North Star directly overhead. Since the stars moved from east to west, it must have been about ten thirty. The house was quiet and dark.

The wind coming from the north was gentle on my back. It felt wonderful, but from where I stood, it put my scenting instinct at a disadvantage. Suddenly I felt a tug at my paw. General Henry was trying to kick me in the shins, which was about as high as he could get.

I had a tremendous urge to step on the little creep. I mean, enough was enough.

But the general wasn't playing games.

His eyes were frantic. He was running

around in circles trying to get my undivided attention without barking.

When I turned to follow him, the wind told me what it had already told him.

Someone was trespassing.

If Maggie and Tom had been home, I would have started barking immediately. Tom would have hit the lights, and whoever was there would have left.

But this was different. In spite of the mixed emotions I had about Henry, I sensed he had reached the same conclusion. Tom was not here; Grammy was. She was propped up in bed to support a twisted back. The next biggest person, Seth, was only ten years old and sixty-five pounds—and Kathleen and Annie weren't exactly first-string backups.

I looked at Henry. He seemed to understand. We would have to do this without human assistance.

There was a distinct familiarity to the scent, but I couldn't place it. We saw the shadow moving in and out of the garage. He was moving quickly, carrying each load to the back of a green van parked under some trees.

We saw no driver. He was alone.

Henry and I plotted our strategy: while Henry distracted the robber, I would close in on him.

The man had only a few more trips before he

finished cleaning out everything—the Hilti screw guns, the B&D drills, the hand saws, the expensive hedge clippers that Tom had found one year by his Christmas stocking.

It made me so mad I forgot to be afraid.

But then I saw the gun. It looked like a bump in the man's vest until he stopped to examine the golf clubs. When he bent over I could see it sticking out.

What if he decided to go into the house? For the TVs or jewelry? What if one of the kids awoke?

Henry hid on the far side of the garage.

I circled around to the front, cowering behind the spruce trees as the man passed me on his way to the van. The North Star cast an eerie glow on his face.

He was the sandy-haired man from the lock shop! He'd heard that Tom was out of town. Seth had even talked about his dad's business. And our address was on the receipt! Then to arrive and find one garage door wide open—it was a piece of cake.

Henry signaled and we started barking. The man didn't know which way to look first, but he finally turned toward the loudest bark, mine.

We had counted on that. We had him between us and we had him confused.

As he stepped back, reaching for his gun,

Henry charged, catching him in the calves and causing him to fall.

The gun fell out of the man's hand, and I pounced on his chest.

Though I had him pinned, I was hoping he wouldn't call my bluff. I bared my teeth in the direction of his throat. It was the greatest bit of acting in my life. I prayed he wouldn't feel my knees shaking.

It worked. Two hundred pounds of still-wet St. Bernard on his chest and a snarling black dachshund at his feet. . . . Well, for his money, we were killer dogs.

I was wondering what to do next when Henry, arrogant as ever, lifted the gun in his paw, twirling it carelessly.

Henry! Whillickers! Don't be dumb! It's surely loaded.

Butch Cassidy he was not.

Booooooooooooooom!

We saw the bullet whiz past the picture window.

If I had wondered what to do next, that cinched it.

The lights went on in the house, pronto.

Chapter 6

We were pretty much blood brothers after that, even on the days we didn't like each other. Henry never mentioned the dish disaster and I never mentioned his stupid showing off with the gun. As far as the family was concerned, we were heroes, and we made the most of this preferred status.

Don't misunderstand me—Henry still was no boy scout. But as the week wore on I got a closer look at why he was the way he was. You see, he didn't have any children to take care of. He only had Grammy. And the fact was, he didn't take care of Grammy. She took care of him.

The morning after the thief incident, Grammy still did not call the doctor. She said her back was one hundred percent better. She was able to straighten up, but I knew it still hurt. Whenever she got up or down she'd call me, and support herself by leaning on my back.

I was glad to help.

I knew she was trying to give Maggie the gift of time.

Seth brought a step stool up from the garage so Grammy could cook sitting down.

Gosh, could she cook.

To my pleasant surprise, Henry's appetite was much too small to threaten my share of leftovers. We ate like kings.

Grammy's biggest problem was keeping up with energetic Annie when Seth and Kathleen were in school. That's when I saw the soft side of Henry.

Henry had this faded orange ball with a peculiar squeaker in it. The noise reminded me of chalk on a blackboard, but Henry loved it. He guarded it like the national treasure. One of the first things he did when he came to our house was to find a suitable hiding place for it—under the middle cushion of the velvet couch.

It so happened that that was the same place Annie picked to stash her Old Maid cards.

Henry was taking a nap in the kitchen when

he heard someone squeak his toy two rooms away.

I never saw him move so fast. Like a black bullet, he shot to the source of the sound.

I went racing after him, afraid for Annie.

Her little voice twinkled to both of us, "Hi, Henny. Hi, Judge. Nice ball. Wanna play?" With that, she rolled the ball to Henry.

He caught it in his mouth and then just stood there. He didn't have another hiding place in mind, and he didn't like the idea of letting it go again.

I was breathing a sigh of relief that he hadn't tried to take it away from Annie when she pranced over to him, pried open his mouth—

pried open his mouth!!!!

—and took the ball away.

"My turn again," she said, giggling, and rolled it back.

Well, now Henry knew firsthand about a little girl's charm.

They played ball several times a day after that. Sometimes Henry actually noticed when Grammy was tired and brought the ball to Annie to start a game.

I tried to join them a couple of times, but Henry gave me a "Get your own ball" look and I settled for the role of spectator.

On the days Henry was in a particularly

sociable mood, the three of us—Henry, Annie, and I—would play hide-and-seek.

Henry always hid in the same dumb spot, the front half of him under the leather chair and the bottom half sticking out, black tail wagging. Maybe it wasn't that dumb. After all, Annie could always find him, and that made her laugh.

I had an even harder time finding a hiding place. I mean, you just don't stash two hundred pounds of St. Bernard behind a magazine rack. It was either under Maggie's bed or behind the big couch.

Once I got tired of the usual spots and tried to curl up under the drop-leaf coffee table.

Dumb.

I squeezed in all right, but I couldn't squeeze out.

Grammy walked in when I made the mistake of standing up. I thought Grammy would never stop laughing.

The table, of course, stayed on my back. My legs were longer than its legs, and the drop-leaf sides stuck on my shoulders. It must have looked like a giant wooden saddle.

Grammy unstuck me, and after that I stopped making fun of Henry's hiding place.

We all missed Maggie and Tom.

Grammy cooked every fattening, desirable

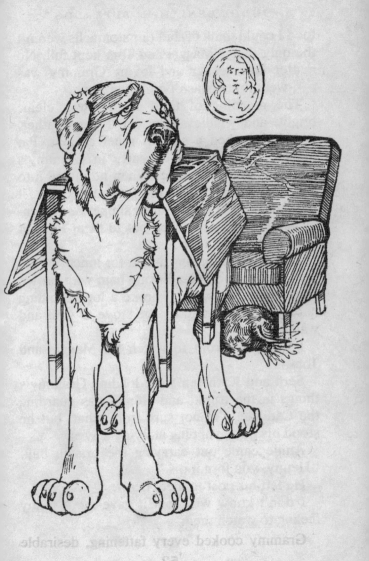

food I could think of, but our stomachs weren't the only things Maggie and Tom kept full. No matter how tender and loving Grammy was . . . well, it just wasn't quite the same.

The morning of their return was clear, bright, and windless—perfect flying weather. We all breathed a sigh of relief at that. Pa, Maggie's father, arrived early in Grammy's marvelous blue Cadillac. When he pulled into the driveway alongside the parked Gremlin, it reminded me of Cinderella's slipper and a tennis shoe. Henry marched out to meet Pa as if he were born to a limousine.

Grammy was baking a ham for lunch. Nothing smells quite like a baking ham with brown sugar and cloves, but I broke a long-standing habit and didn't stay by the stove to sniff and wait.

I went out front to watch for Maggie and Tom.

Seth and Kathleen were loading Grammy's things in the trunk, and Henry was guarding the Cadillac. I'm not sure from what, but he stood his post, yapping at flying leaves.

Annie came out carrying the orange ball. "Henny, you forgot dis."

He left his post to meet her.

I don't know why, but it gave me a funny feeling to watch them.

Annie put her hand out with the ball, and he took it from her.

"You're fun, Henny. You play good."

It could have gotten very sloppy and sentimental, but just then Maggie and Tom pulled in the drive.

After five minutes of hugging and kissing, it was as if they had never left.

The lunch was glorious, even though everyone was talking at once. I don't know how humans manage that. With all that good food it seems a waste of an open mouth. Henry ate with the little orange ball just inches from his nose.

Pa stood up, finally, saying they must go if they hoped to get home before dark.

Maggie cried when she hugged Grammy, and that set off a chain reaction you wouldn't have believed.

Eventually, Grammy and Pa made it to their car, closed the trunk, and got in.

Not Henry. He was standing next to Annie, still holding that dumb ball.

"Henry, c'mon," Grammy coaxed.

The car door was open and everybody waited. Little as Henry was, no one was about to pick him up against his will.

"Henry, we're going to stop and get ice cream," Pa suggested.

Henry didn't move.

Annie had been sizing up the situation. Even in her little girl eyes she knew that Henry belonged to Grammy. She got down on her knees and planted a generous kiss on Henry's little black nose. "You c'n come back soon, Henny."

I guess that was all he needed. Henry headed for the car, turned back once, dropped the scrungy orange ball by Annie's foot, and hopped into his car bed.

He would be back.

When they were just a short way down the road, I saw Henry barking at a squirrel that had dared to come within twenty feet of *his* car.

Maggie gave me a big hug as we made our way back to the house. She noticed how tight my collar was. "Judge Benjamin! Too much gravy and desserts?"

I knew I'd strayed from sensible eating long enough. Maggie put me on a diet of Gainesburgers and eggs for a month. She even cut out my morning cereal.

But I didn't mind too much.

I had my kingdom back. As much as Henry and I had done together, I was grateful as heck not to have to listen to *"Hronksha!"* one more night.

Chapter 7

It was getting close to the end of winter when the high dry fronts of February began pushing through Decatur. By Valentine's Day—I knew that was coming because Annie Elizabeth chose the occasion to plaster my body with Elmer's glue–stuck hearts—I figured the mild winter was on its way out.

Maggie had blossomed in the manner of pregnant ladies, and all of us were working overtime to make things easier for her. She had had firm orders from her doctor not to overdo. So Seth vacuumed, Kathleen did most of the laundry, and I kept Annie entertained. Tom did some of the cooking.

During Tom's first week of pitching in, I lost eleven pounds.

His soup should have been on exhibit in the Museum of Science and Industry. I watched him sacrifice a gorgeous hunk of bone and marrow in his beef broth, and it took my breath away. He didn't bother to peel the onions and the carrots, but in the stew they went. He couldn't find any canned tomatoes (they were right behind the peas), so he added a bottle of barbecue sauce. He selected two green peppers and a handful of bay leaves for more flavor.

My tummy flipflopped.

After that, I couldn't watch.

We emptied two boxes of Saltines and a gallon of milk washing that soup down.

Tom's French toast would better have been called the dish without a country. He found a loaf of rye bread and decided to use it up. When mixing the eggs, he grabbed the buttermilk by mistake. He couldn't seem to get the temperature of the griddle regulated on the electric stove, and the bread took on the color of a Hershey's kiss. He thought he was sprinkling powdered sugar on top, but it was selfrising flour, and when he added the carefully heated syrup—his good intentions were superior—great white blobs formed on the peculiar toast.

Maggie dug up a box of graham crackers and the early bird milkman left an extra gallon of milk.

Three nights of dried, greasy, and raw hamburgers later—in that order—there was a most unusual parade to the pantry.

I watched from a front-and-center spot under the kitchen table.

Annie Elizabeth was first.

She was wearing the pink hand-me-down sleepers with the bunny patches on the knees and those slippery footies. She wasn't tall enough to reach the light, so she grabbed a couple of familiar-shaped boxes and joined me under the table.

One was raisins.

No problem. I even got two for my companionship.

The next was a little trickier; macaroni and cheese. Getting it open was a challenge, but Annie was up to it. When banging it on the floor didn't help, she found a Lincoln Log and stabbed it to death. The flying dry macaroni made little crinkly noises rolling on the floor and I was sure she'd be discovered, but no one came.

Annie was quite disappointed when she popped a piece and found it was not like the picture on the box.

Bleah.

She settled for the dried cheese packet, which she opened with her teeth and poured down like Kool-Aid.

Then Maggie came.

She had gone to tuck Annie in and guessed correctly when she couldn't find her.

As I lay there surrounded by hundreds of raw noodles, I wondered about my defense. It turned out neither Annie nor I needed any.

"Oh, you poor things," Maggie sighed. She made four peanut butter and jelly sandwiches for Annie and me to share, and cleaned up the mess without another word.

Minutes later, Kathleen and Seth tiptoed in.

"Mom, we're kinda hungry," Kathleen whispered.

"I know. There seems to be a lot of that going around." Maggie made four more sandwiches and peeled a banana for herself.

Seth wolfed down three, and Kathleen didn't even give me her crust.

This was getting serious.

We sat there, the five of us, on the floor by the pantry with just a sliver of light cutting through the kitchen. We all knew what each was thinking. Finally, there was a whispered discussion.

Naturally, it was Kathleen who broke the ice. "Mom, what are we going to do? It's nice Dad is trying to help, but we're starving to death!"

Seth started on a banana. "Boy, you said it.

A couple more *yech* menus and I'll fade away."

"Don't talk with your mouth full," Kathleen scolded. "We'd never get that lucky."

"Shhh, kids," said Maggie. "Don't fuss. We don't want to wake Dad. I know we have a problem, but I tried, and there's just no changing Dad's mind without hurting his feelings."

"Mom," Kathleen said, "remember the cooking badge in my *Girl Scout Handbook*? We said we'd work on that over the summer. Suppose we told Dad that I needed to start it now."

"Gad! It's bad enough to have to put up with Dad's cooking. Kathleen would poison us for sure!" growled Seth.

"Now, Seth, Kathleen may have a good idea," said Maggie. "Kathleen, you have so much to do already. . . . That's why I suggested waiting till summer."

"Oh, heck," Seth offered. "Let's just lay in lots of fruit and peanut butter and meet in the pantry every night."

Annie's head was nodding against mine and her banana was weaving toward my mouth. Maggie got it before I did.

"No, we need our sleep, too. Actually, Kathleen's idea appeals to me. We can make double batches of whatever she has to fix, freeze half, and get a little ahead of Dad.

Suppose we divide the menus a bit, so he won't suspect. Let Dad oversee the salads, I'll watch Kathleen do most of the main courses, and you, Seth, can have a hand at desserts."

"Don't give Seth anything harder than dishing out ice cream, Mom," Kathleen said. "Remember how Seth cooked the eggs before adding them to the brownies one time?"

"Now, Kathleen, you and Seth both learned a lot from those first cooking experiences. I think we should try it."

Seth and Kathleen exchanged looks. They knew they had to make a choice: truce or starve. They were resigned.

"Dad will still feel like helping out." Maggie sighed. "The plan won't resolve that."

"Maybe he and I can build something for the baby," Seth said.

"I don't know what. By the time you get to number-four child, you have everything you need. The cradle could stand refinishing, though. . . ."

"Why don't we paint the spare bedroom?" Seth suggested.

"I know, we can—" Kathleen stopped in mid-sentence. "*Shhh!* He's coming. Dad's coming! If he finds out we've been here pigging out after that terrible supper, he'll be crushed."

Maggie was picking up the banana peels and

milk carton. "Quick!" she instructed. "Hide in the pantry!"

Seth scooped up the dozing Annie.

Now, I'm not sure why I chose to join the rest of them. I often sleep under the kitchen table, so there would have been nothing suspicious about that. But I guess I got caught in the flurry of things. Anyway, when the four of them pulled the light off and flattened themselves against the flour, cereals, and what-have-you, I went charging right along with them. When my nose wound up within an inch of the cooking oil and Karo syrup, I stopped short, just at the instant Seth reached behind me to pull the door shut.

Seth couldn't have known. It was pitch dark. But six inches of St. Bernard tail hadn't quite made it into the pantry.

The pain was tremendous.

I heard Tom thumping into the room with the same rhythm my heart was pounding.

My eyes began to water.

I was sure the flow of blood had been cut off forever. I stood it for almost two full minutes before the howl finally pulled free from my clenched teeth.

It accompanied my body crashing through the pantry door and landing at Tom's feet.

Tom almost choked on his Pepto-Bismol.

Chapter 8

Tom's pride and my tail both healed.

In fact, Tom's good nature—and the frequent hearty doses of indigestion that his own cooking had caused—saw the plan for what it was: salvation.

When Kathleen presented her cooking badge idea, Tom agreed without a fuss. He even confessed to the hoard of empty Milky Way wrappers he had stashed in the glove compartment since becoming head O'Riley chef. When it came to a choice between Tom's pride and Tom's appetite, there was no contest.

I could identify with that.

Under the new rules, Maggie agreed to keep her feet elevated throughout the dinner preparation. This was so she wouldn't have to jump up every few minutes to find the vanilla, sharpen a knife, or clean up a spill. It gave her swollen feet a rest. She planned the meals with Kathleen, and together they made the assignments.

Tom was a real sport. He never complained about boiling water for the Jell-O, chopping eggs for a salad, or heating caramel sauce for a dessert. I was sure he knew why he was handed the easy chores.

Seth and Kathleen pulled out all the competitive stops and did a great job. Maggie kept the meals simple but filling. They started with easy menus, like scrambled eggs and a garden salad. Then they mastered simple stews, chili, and casseroles. Soon hot dogs and hamburgers became the exception, not the rule. Annie helped by setting the table and taking out the garbage.

When the new routine became a matter of course, phase two of getting ready for the new baby took shape. One Saturday, the dump-everything room became a nursery.

Maggie was directing junk traffic like a New York policeman. "Don't take that box, Seth, it has baby things."

Tom pulled Annie out of a box of books. She was squealing with pleasure and managed to hang onto an old dictionary. She proceeded to read to me while the others worked. When she didn't think I was paying sufficient attention, she would take my nose in her chubby hands and push it firmly into the book.

It was amazing. There wasn't one color picture in that ancient edition, but Annie made up an incredible story about two Dracumonsters, whatever they are.

"Mom, where did all this junk come from?" Kathleen was dusting a battered floor lamp minus a shade.

"Careful, dear, you're talking about our Early American Attic donations. We couldn't have managed without them."

"You did call Goodwill for a pickup?" Tom was sorting a pile of suitcases to store on racks in the garage.

"They'll be here tomorrow, but I still hate to part with some of this. The memories!"

"Now, Maggie, what would you have us do, sleep standing up so we'd have room to save everything?"

"Hey, would you look at this?" Seth was holding up a football jersey the size of one of my ears. "Don't tell me I wore this!"

"You did. You crawled to the ends of your little world wearing that. Maybe a little brother will have the same experience," Maggie said.

"Brother! *Yech!* Double Creemo Jeemo! This baby is going to be a girl!" Kathleen was trying to convince everyone, including herself.

"C'mon. Dad and I are outnumbered already. It's only fair that this one be a boy."

Seth could have counted me.

Annie put down her book when the subject came up.

"I want a gog. Jus' like Judge. A puppygog."

That Annie had taste.

"Oh, dear!" Maggie sighed. "Where have I gone wrong?"

"I'll tell you what," Tom offered. "Suppose I go out and buy a pair of boy-girl puppies."

I breathed a sigh of relief when everyone began to laugh. For a minute I wasn't sure if he was kidding.

It took hours to clean the room and get it ready for painting.

"No, Kathleen, pink is not a practical choice," Tom said firmly. "It could be a son."

"But it's going to be a girl, Dad. It's absolutely, positively, definitely, almost certain!" Kathleen's voice got a little higher in pitch.

"What's wrong with blue? Girls and boys both like blue," Seth said.

"Well, it's not exactly a neutral color, big brother."

"Burple. Burple and orange and pink," Annie contributed.

"Hold it, kids," Maggie said. "It's not up for votes. Dad is picking up Sunshine Yellow at

68

the hardware store, which just happens to be next to McDonald's, and it's lunchtime.''

Maggie had an instinct for peace.

They brought home two Big Macs for me. Wonderful! I'm not crazy about lettuce, but the sesame seeds and that sauce! I really liked that.

Tom rented a large tarpaulin to protect the hardwood floor, and Kathleen and Seth brought in the ladder, paint cans, rollers, and brushes. Maggie gathered a tyke bike, a few little cars, and a bag labeled Potential Genius. She brought Annie and me out back on the patio and gave explicit instructions.

First she whispered to me, ''Judge, you keep a close eye on Annie. I'll lock the gate for you.'' . . . and then to Annie . . . ''Now, honey, Judge Benjamin can't help us paint, so your job is to keep him company. Why don't you collect some nice rocks in your bag here?''

She gave Annie a hug and a kiss and patted my shoulder for a minute before going in. She came out back once to check the lock on the gate, and smiled at Annie, who was building a mud house on my paw.

''Good boy, Judge. The patience of a saint, right?'' She laughed at her own little joke and went back inside, confident that all was well.

All was well—for a bit.

The sun kept trying to peek through those gray February clouds, and a cool, dry breeze gently lifted the long hair on my back. Sitting very still for Annie's artwork required relaxing and, though I fought it, I dozed off.

When I awoke, I saw two red and yellow sneakers squeezing through a loose board in the fence and heading for parts unknown.

I wasn't quick enough to stop her. The bouncy blond ponytail escaped down the hill, dragging the Potential Genius canvas bag. I dismally watched her deposit sticks and weeds and any treasures she found along the way.

The loose board that had given way to free Annie wasn't much wider than my paw. I couldn't get through. I pawed at the gate, but the lock was too sturdy to break. I tried to dig at some of the soft ground to squeeze under the fence, but it would take too long.

I began to bark, my deepest panic bark. They had to come out.

Nothing.

I could hear them laughing and talking and singing "Jingle Bells."

"Jingle Bells?" In February?

Probably the only song Tom knew.

Again and again I barked.

"Cut it out, Judge," Tom yelled out the window. "We'll be finished in another half hour, and then we'll start supper."

70

He didn't understand and I couldn't make him. My biggest emergencies were usually hunger pains, and I had cried "Wolf!" once too often.

I looked under the fence. Annie had moved on down the hill, nearer to the street.

She sat herself down at the drainage ditch near the water pipe and was examining an odd green rock.

I couldn't wait a half hour.

I tried to hurl myself over the fence, but my center of gravity kept pulling me down. Twice I got halfway over. I needed someone or something to boost my back paws. I tried the chaise longue but, besides being too short, my paws slipped right through the webbing and I wasted precious time getting untangled.

The patio table was too heavy for me to move.

It wasn't a safe plan, but it seemed to me the only plan. I moved the picnic bench up against the fence and put the tyke bike on top of that. Graceful I was not, but I shot for it. It wasn't a very delicate acrobatic stunt, and I heard the tyke bike sail out from under me just as I got the boost I needed to land outside the fence. I got between Annie and the street a lot more deftly than I somersaulted over the fence.

Annie was easily persuaded to head back to the house. She climbed on the milk box to reach the door knob, and when she turned it and pulled the door a fraction, I got my paw in position to pull it open the rest of the way. I thought our troubles were over.

Little did I imagine.

Annie marched in holding the Potential Genius bag with her collection in front of her. I had hoped to head her off to her room, but she wasn't about to be led. From my trailing position, I heard a noise.

"Ribbit."

Ribbit? Highly suspect.

"Ribbit. Ribbit."

My heart skipped a beat. Rocks don't go around spouting "Ribbit."

Frantically, I skipped around Annie to make a grab for the bag. Annie giggled and took off. She thought it was a game and headed for the nursery to recruit more players.

The paint job was in the final stages—I could see that from my position in the hall. Maggie was kneeling on the floor, finishing the trim under the window. Kathleen was on the ladder catching the corner of trim near the ceiling. Seth was finishing up with the roller on the main wall. In the middle of the floor, Tom was cleaning extra brushes and getting the paint cans together to be capped.

Annie entered the room, smiling and coy. "Mom, lookeeee!"

Too late, I slid in behind her.

Annie had opened the bag and two frogs came out ribbiting.

For an instant the O'Rileys froze.

Maybe the paint cans with the yellow goo reminded the frogs of a lily pad, because that's where they headed first.

Kathleen broke the freeze with a scream. *"Yeaach! Frogs!* I can't breathe!"

I'm not sure what breathing had to do with it, but her screeching continued.

Tom reached for the hopping frogs and got a yellow nose for his efforts. Seth tried to attack them with the paint roller. Maggie, in her pregnant state, never got off her knees, but kept swaying back and forth trying to grab them as they jumped by. Annie was laughing. "Frog-geeees! Wheeeeeee!"

I was really exasperated. Tom was giving me a stern look as if I had engineered the whole stunt. In an instant of timing that I'll never understand, I reached to catch one with my paw, missed, opened my mouth to bark, and . . .

Bingo. The top half of the frog took roost in my soft mouth and I felt two green feet dangling past my chin.

With a calm that matched my own quiet state of shock, Annie walked up to the other now-

74

frightened, tired frog, picked him up, and made her way to Kathleen. "See! I found 'em all by myself! Don't you jus' luf it!"

Kathleen's scream could be heard around the world.

Later when Tom deposited the frogs in the back yard—I wondered what their friends thought of the yellow polka dots—Tom found the tyke bike lodged in a rose bush. He gave a curious look at the out-of-place picnic bench and, with a little more investigation, found the loose board. He couldn't put the pieces together exactly, but he decided I'd responded above and beyond the call of duty, in spite of the paint mishap.

My favor knew no bounds. I was patted, praised, and given a half gallon of ice cream for my loyalty and protectiveness. In fact, I was feeling quite cocky.

The mess in the nursery had been tidied up by bedtime and, when everyone else was tucked in, I decided to have a last look.

It was quite inviting.

The yellow paint gave the small room a softness that outlined like sunshine the newly finished oak furnishings. The largest wall behind the Jenny Lind bed was filled with brightly colored pictures that a baby would love. The dresser and dressing table were already packed with the layette. On a small blue oriental rug in the very center of the room the cradle stood—the tenderly handed-down heirloom that would be the baby's first resting place.

I lay down beside it, remembering the first time. I had been but a puppy when I learned that, by gently touching my paw to the curved runner, I could rock a cooing child into soft sleep. I thought of the littleness, the incredible perfection in baby fingers and toes.

Maggie had a clean receiving blanket already in place, and in my imagination I could almost see a new little girl or boy waiting to be rocked.

Very gently I put my nose between the rungs to count the Pooh Bears in the pattern on the blanket and dream of the O'Riley soon to be born. I could almost smell the clean baby smell and hear Maggie's lullaby.

When I finally tried to get up and call it a night, I realized it wasn't a clean baby smell that had sifted through my nostrils.

It was varnish.

And it was still tacky between the rungs.

I couldn't pull my nose out! Moreover, by standing up, my body and the cradle formed a large T that wouldn't go through the doorway.

I had two options.

I could wake the rest of the house so that Tom could rescue me with a spot of turpentine and a scolding. Or I could stay put, be discovered in the morning, and be a hero for a few hours longer.

What was there to decide?

This was the best place to dream of babies anyway.

Chapter 9

It was the third sunrise of April and I arose with the first touch of morning. I padded through the house checking on all that was mine to guard.

"Judge Benjamin, are you up already? It can't be that time."

Maggie was mumbling into the pillow, trying to avoid the nice wet kiss I saved for her. She wasn't responding to my morning hello at all. "Gimme a break, Judge. Just five more minutes."

Five more minutes and she would regret it. She knew I had to go out. I decided she needed a few more wet kisses.

"I give up! I give up!"

I had thought she would.

Maggie rolled out lumpily and rubbed my back. Then she grabbed her bathrobe, which went on inside out with the inspected by #29 sticker tickling my ear. She kept reaching for the sash as she walked down the hall and through the kitchen before she realized her mistake.

"Some little fairy must have come in and changed this. It was right side when I took it off last night. Come on, big fella, let's catch that guy one of these nights."

Poor Maggie. She had been so tired these last few months of pregnancy that she was usually half asleep before she even crawled into bed at night.

We passed the refrigerator long enough for Maggie to grab my bowl of milk. She slid it onto the back stoop. I hinted for a couple of doughnuts, and she plunked two in my open mouth.

I was off for the apple trees.

I chewed slowly, the powdered sugar melting on my tongue and driving out all evil thoughts of a diet tomorrow.

After a few quiet moments, the day began— the clump of the paper at the front door, the ring of first-shift whistles in the distance, the noisy sparrows gathering in their skylight nest.

I arose to stake out the property, and was somewhat puzzled by the day's lack of dew. I regularly washed my face in it, shaking off its pleasant coolness and drying in the sun.

Had I overslept?

No, right on schedule I noted by the sun. And it wasn't what you would call a muggy morning.

But no dew. Funny.

I studied the sky for more weather signals, but there was nothing else unusual.

My knock at the back door caught Maggie mopping up Annie's spilled milk, a job I would gladly have taken had I been on the spot. It was Kathleen who let me in.

I adored watching Kathleen. While the rest of the family spent early morning as if they were walking in wet sand, Kathleen fairly flew. She was the first dressed, the first to make her bed, the first to chatter cheerfully.

"Judge, you're all shedding. Why do you do that? And there's powdered sugar on your nose. Mom, has he had doughnuts already?"

Doughnuts are one of the great joys of my life, Kathleen. I have often thought of jogging, but something always happens to my good intentions.

"And you chatter too much, Kathleen. The Judge gets hungry same as you, and there is a lot more of him to fill up. Give me a hand setting the table, will you? Then I can have the dishwasher unloaded before I sit down. Where's Seth? He did get up, didn't he?''

Oh, he got up. One finger, one toe at a time.

Kathleen was ready with the tattle. "He's still combing his hair and it's my comb."

I had wondered recently about Seth's new interest in his appearance. Until about two weeks ago, he only stayed in front of the bathroom mirror long enough to spit toothpaste on it. Well, we could bet Kathleen would keep us informed if Cupid pointed an arrow in Seth's direction.

"Kathleen, instead of complaining, why don't you get the cereal?"

Good. Cold with milk, the way I like it. I was hoping it wouldn't be one of those oversweetened excuses for nutrition. I saw Maggie pull out the shredded wheat. Good choice.

Maggie surely was moving slower these days. Annie hadn't slept well because of a touch of flu, and that meant neither had Maggie. So the wheels of the morning meal were grinding slowly.

Ah, but then Tom entered.

"Good morning, family!"

While the chaos had built to a peak and finally played itself out, Tom had finished a hot shower and arrived at the fully set table looking quite clean and pressed.

Maggie disappeared into the pantry to flick a comb through her hair and grab a bit of lipstick, then sat down.

Everyone held hands for grace, and each took his turn with the special "thank you" to his Maker.

"You first, Seth."

"Thank you for doughnuts."

"You say that every morning."

"Now, Kathleen, just take your turn."

"Thank you for ribbons."

"Your turn, Annie."

"Thank you for . . ."—the ultimate pause—"pluffs."

"Pluffs?"

"She has a cold. She means tissues."

A roar broke out at the table.

Maggie thanked God for laughter, and Tom thanked God that he would be leaving for the office soon. He was still laughing when Maggie gave him one of those married frowns that lasted about a tenth of a second before it too melted into a chuckle.

I sat directly beneath Annie's chair and at right angles to Seth and Kathleen, and was duly rewarded with bits of doughnuts and wedges of fruit. Maggie had been too busy to

peel the apples, so I had to manage myself, and by the time breakfast was over, bits of red skin littered the floor. Maggie wasn't going to be too happy about that so, for the time being, I lay my head down and tucked them under my chin.

"Must you go out of town today, Tom?"

"I'm afraid so. I have to pick up a set of plans in East St. Louis."

"But that's so far!"

"I can be home in an hour and a half, and Dr. Lacey said you probably won't deliver for three weeks."

"I guess I'll have to keep the kids out of school one more day. The throat culture report won't be available until noon."

"They look fine, Maggie."

"I know, but it isn't fair to the rest of the students. They might catch it. Strep throat can be deceiving."

"Whatever you think is best."

There followed the silent facial applause of Seth, who would gladly have skipped school for a hangnail, and the tearful woes of Kathleen, who was sure she wouldn't survive a day without it.

"Will you try to call?"

"Maggie, I can't promise. You know how hectic work is some days."

"Mom, can we at least go by school and pick up my workbook?"

"Kathleen, it's probably just one more day. You have your reader and your math book, and. . . ."

"Please, Mom. I just have to!"

"What books do *you* need, Seth?"

"Oh, umm, I'm pretty caught up, Mom."

Right. Seth was probably caught up in volleyball and art and library books. Good thinking, Seth.

"Annie can run in with a note to your teachers and pick up *both* of your books. I'll take her by school after lunch."

Seth melted into the chair. Darn that Kathleen. Homework was something he could live without.

I had been so intent watching and listening that I lifted my chin to study the situation. . . .

"Judge Benjamin!"

Rats.

"Look at that mess!"

Caught.

Tom very tactfully began to ease his chair out. "I think I'd best be off, Maggie."

Good idea. It would take some of the pressure off me. I could sneak out back. The wooden door was open, and I could manage the handle on the storm door, so outsville.

"I think that animal is more trouble than all the kids," I heard Maggie say.

"Now, Maggie, you know you think the world of him." Tom was always on my team.

But even so, I was going to have to redeem myself before the day was over.

Chapter 10

I plodded around out back, long enough to miss the mushies. There was a lot of kissing and hugging at the door that didn't really require my presence. When I returned, Maggie was making stew, one of my favorites.

I forgot earlier thoughts about recovering my waistline and planted my two hundred pounds in the spot between the stove and the refrigerator, where the goodies would most likely fall. Then, in one swift arc of my fat paw, I could steer them into my waiting mouth. At this I had become a master. Maggie put up with it, even though she did tease me about the apple skins from breakfast.

It was still bothering me about the lack of dew. When the meat and vegetables were cut and layered in the Crock-Pot, I went for another walk out back.

Jet contrails all right, which meant a warm moist front headed our way. Some cirrus clouds, lots of stratus clouds, but no signs of real activity yet. I had a feeling though, a kind of pressure I couldn't explain. I remembered stories my mother had told me about my great-great-great-grandfather and how he could sense an avalanche hours before it happened. But that was silly. Nothing like an avalanche could happen here in Decatur, Illinois. What was I thinking?

After a while, Maggie came out to sweep the patio. She was stooping a bit, favoring her back. I didn't like the looks of it. The sweeping wasn't that necessary, but her health was, so I did my part by walking up and knocking the broom down. Then I rolled over on the broom so she had to quit.

"Judge Benjamin! For crying out loud!"

The broom was digging into my shoulders, but I had to stay that way until she made up her mind to sit.

"Oh, all right, I'll sit with you a minute, Judge."

Maggie went straight for the lounge chair and put her feet up where they belonged. I went over, putting my head on her lap so she would scratch behind my ears.

The sky was beginning to cloud up a bit more—puffy, fat clouds that meant rain. They were moving pretty fast, maybe fifteen, sixteen miles an hour. Odd. That would be normal with a cold front, but not with the warm moist air I presumed was on its way. Something was not exactly right, but I couldn't put my paw on it.

It felt good just sitting there quietly, keeping Maggie company and watching the clouds. But quiet moments are always brief. We could hear mumbles of a sibling argument from inside.

A chorus of *"Mom"* came running out the back door, followed by "She started it!" "He started it!" "They started it!"

"Shhh, kids, look at that giant white cloud." The pleas stopped.

"I'm going to give you each two guesses what you think I think it is. Let's start with the youngest. Annie?"

"Ahhh . . . uhhhh . . . ahhhh . . . a meatball."

"That's not such a bad idea; it's round. But no. Guess again."

"Ummmm . . . ahhh . . . the White House."

Seth's chin dropped six inches. "The White House!? What do you know about the White House?"

"That's what color Julie's house was 'fore her daddeeee painted it. She tol' me."

Annie got a big hug from Maggie on that one.

"All right, Kathleen, your turn."

"Lace for a wedding dress."

Seth dramatically hid his eyes with his hand, but he stopped short of telling Kathleen it was dumb.

"Oh, I like that guess," Maggie said. "But, no. One more, Kathleen."

"A giant marshmallow."

"No fair, that was going to be my guess!" yelled Seth.

"Well, it isn't right. Do you still want it to be your guess?"

"No."

"Okay, Seth. Then go ahead."

The pause was considerable.

"Well, I was so sure I was going to be right with the marshmallow that I didn't think of anything else. But I'm thinking now!"

Kathleen was biting back her "silly brother" routine.

"I've got it. It's a vanilla sundae with marshmallow sauce and whipped cream and coconut sprinkles," said Seth finally.

"Yummy, but no."

"What's for lunch?"

It was obvious that Seth was no longer concerned about the competition.

"It's only ten thirty. Finish your turn."

"A dish of tapioca without the cherry. Are you sure it's only ten thirty?"

"I'm sure. And no. The answer to the riddle about what do I think the cloud is? It's a good way to stop an argument that Mother doesn't want to make a ruling on."

Seth appeared in pain. "*Aaaagh!* We've been had!"

The fat cloud that had commanded everyone's attention was long gone when Maggie went in to fix lunch. In fact, the whole crowd of tufts was gradually being replaced by bigger clouds, closer together and not as cheerful looking. But they were not yet really gray, and I hesitated to make a judgment on an empty stomach, so I went in to eat.

Chapter 11

At Seth's request, lunch was early—eleven thirty to be exact. When Maggie reached up to put the hot dogs in the microwave, she grabbed the small of her back and closed her eyes.

I had a feeling this wasn't just a twinge.

But the timer went off and she took the hot dogs out, gave me my usual pat on the head, and served up lunch without a complaint.

Microwave hot dogs are one of those special little pleasures, plump and juicy. Maggie always fixed two for me, but I hung around hoping no one else was hungry and I might get more. As it turned out, Maggie barely tasted hers. For some reason, I felt a little wicked eating it. She surely looked tired.

When Maggie was dishing up ice cream and

cookies for the clean-plate kids—I was always one of those—the clinic called. The lab report on the throat culture was good. The inflammation was not caused by strep infection.

"Kathleen, you and Seth can go back to school tomorrow, so Annie and I are not going to make a trip to school today just to pick up a workbook."

"Oh, *Mom!*"

"No, it's not necessary, Kathleen, and . . . and to tell the truth, I'm not feeling very well."

I was glad she'd decided that. It seemed she wasn't telling us everything, but I figured she had her reasons. Kathleen must have sensed something too, because she didn't say anything more, even with Seth kicking her under the table and grinning like crazy.

When Maggie excused herself, I followed her into the bedroom and heard one side of a very brief telephone conversation that was preceded by another one of those pauses, eyes closed, holding her back.

"This is Mrs. O'Riley. I'm not due for several weeks, but I am experiencing some pains on and off. . . ."

I knew it!

". . . and I thought I'd better check with the doctor. . . . Oh, he's not. Well, I'm sure there's no hurry but, considering the complications

94

before, I thought it was best to keep you posted."

It's going to be all right, it's going to be all right—I started pacing the hall outside the bedroom. Calm down, I told myself. I was behaving like my old friend Henry before a pounce. *Geeez!* There would be plenty of time for that later.

"Right. . . . Of course. . . . I'll phone in a couple of hours and let you know. Thanks so much."

Maggie was pulling her overnight bag out of the closet and checking its contents. False alarm or not, she was getting ready, and I was becoming excited. I decided to go out back before I gave her secret away.

The blue was gone from the sky, and I didn't like it. Decatur had all kinds of thunderstorms in April and May, but this one seemed to be shaping up awfully fast. What was that old saying about babies coming with the storm? Let's see, there had been a real blizzard when Kathleen was born, and Annie, too—but it snowed pretty much all the time between October and March in Rockford, where we lived then.

Well, at least a little rain couldn't keep you from getting to the hospital on time, could it?

Then why was I getting so nervous?

Maybe what I needed was a quiet nap under the kitchen table.

Kathleen let me in.

Seth had set up the Monopoly game on the kitchen table after the children had cleared their places from lunch. Annie couldn't really play, but they appointed her banker and then gave her careful instructions on each move. Annie wasn't exactly happy about it, but it was either that or give in to an afternoon nap, so she put up with the situation.

Kathleen brought it up. "Did Mom look okay to you?"

"What do you mean?"

"Do you get your ten hunnert for passing Go now?"

"It's two hundred. No, probably next roll. Oh, you know, kinda tired and funny."

"Of course she's tired. Annie had her up three times last night."

"Did not."

"Did too."

"Not."

"Too."

"Please, guys, stop kidding around. I think Mom is sick. Maybe even going to have the baby today."

"Oh, Kathleen, what do you know?"

"Okay, I don't know. But she is acting

96

funny. Do you suppose she went in to call Grammy to come?"

"Aw, that's just like a girl to jump to conclusions."

"All right, smarty, but if she does, am I ever going to say I told you so!"

Seth was putting up a good front, but I could see he was concerned too. Maybe even a little scared. After all, Tom was out of town, and even though he'd said he would be back in plenty of time, what if he wasn't?

"Are the pink ones fives or five hunnerts?"

"Fives. See, there're no zeroes after the five. Your roll, Seth."

I couldn't concentrate on the game or ignore it enough to get a good nap going, so I went to the big picture window to gaze. I noticed the birds were pretty noisy.

I watched them come and go. They seemed a bit more excited than usual.

Maybe it was just my imagination. At any rate, I chose to make rounds out back again and see for myself.

There was a stillness that just didn't feel right. Above, the clouds seemed to be traveling by layers, not all in the same direction at the same time. It wasn't that movement that bothered me. It was something else.

When I raised my head and breathed deeply,

it was as if my paws were cooler than my ears. And the ground was dry.

I had an awful headache.

Then I remembered something the Lockleys' collie, Jacoby, once said. He was a show dog, and he was pretty sure he knew all there was to know about every possible subject. I never did buy that, but every now and then he would spout off a little tidbit that seemed to make sense.

Jacoby had been at a show in Arkansas, and his trainer was having a heck of a time grooming his coat. The hair just didn't want to separate. It kept matting together. They were at one of the hilly spots in the state, and when they finally gave up on the combing and walked to the bottom of the hill, the air got noticeably cooler. His trainer, rather than being pleased, got nervous. He called it "inversion" when the temperature of air increases with height. It was a warning of severe weather, the eye of a front.

I had been at the far corner of the yard and was running faster than I knew I could when the first drops of rain began to fall. They were big fat drops, very warm at first, but after a few minutes they cooled off. In fact, they began to feel almost cold.

When I got to the back stoop the rain slowed, almost stopped, but then got lighter, heavier.

I was still banging at the door when I noticed the rusty glow the clouds were wearing.

"Okay, Judge, I'm coming."

It was Seth and, big as he was getting to be, I almost knocked him down in my haste to get inside. It wasn't just a knowledge of the weather. It was an instinct—I can't say what, but I knew I had to get my family somewhere safe. It must have been about two o'clock, though I couldn't be certain with the sun behind the clouds.

Maggie was opening and closing the windows, going from one side of the house to the other, trying to keep up with the sudden crazy wind changes that brought the rain in.

"Well, what's all the excitement, Judge?"

It was an Academy Award performance, if I do say so myself. I jumped. I shook my head. I pranced. I nudged her hand. I was Lassie gone wild.

At first she acted amused. Then, very suddenly, she grabbed her back again. When she opened her eyes she began to take me seriously, looking at the windows, the clouds, the rain that had stopped as quickly as it began.

Suddenly, Maggie knew, too.

"Kids, take yourselves to the basement immediately and don't stop for anything. You can finish the game later."

I couldn't believe it, but they never asked

why. They knew the look on Maggie's face meant business, and that was good enough for them.

"Go to the alcove under the main stairs and don't move. I'll be there in a minute."

I watched them from the top of the stairs and waited for Maggie.

But she didn't come.

She was having another pain, and it looked like a humdinger. When it was over, instead of heading for the basement she was going to the linen closet and grabbing some towels. A shower? At a time like this?

Had I been a little smarter I would have known. When I went to hurry her along, I slipped on a very warm wet spot on the kitchen floor. When I sniffed, I could smell the faintness of ammonia, or something like that. . . . My word! It was her bag of waters! There was nothing false about this labor.

I don't know how I knew the storm was going to be bad, but I did. It was a kind of pressure inside my head that I had never felt before. Looking out the window, I could see the low-flying birds and the field rabbits running like crazy for the shelter of the house foundation. It was coming, and there would never be time to make the basement. Maggie was just a step from the bathroom near the middle hall, and I opted for that.

I'm sure I did not walk or run, but flew. I pushed her down beside the tub. As best I could, I shielded her body with mine, and she lay, protecting her unborn.

The noise was intense, like a giant rail car roaring in the bedroom next to us.

And then it hit.

Tornado!

Chapter 12

It was unbelievable. The noise, the whirring, the scattering of furniture like so many pretzels, the little explosions of bursting walls.

In all my life, I had never been called upon to use such strength, but for those few short minutes, I summoned the reserves of my whole spirit. One paw braced against the doorway, one paw slammed against the wall, and the rest of me clinging to I don't know what—the grooves, I guess, on the ceramic floor.

Maggie was trembling and so was I.

But we held on. And when it stopped, the silence was as loud as the noise had been.

We waited a couple of minutes, not really believing such a storm could be over.

It was then that we heard the siren—a shrill,

long honk designed by the city of Decatur to warn of disaster. It could be heard plainly, even where we were.

When I finally got up, my legs were weak and stiff. I had strained more than I thought, but I got them moving and nudged Maggie to do the same.

"Judge, the children, check the children!"

She was struggling a bit to get up with me. She looked very weak. There was a small gash over her left eye, which must have been hit by some flying fragment. But other than that. . . .

"I'm fine, Judge. I'll be along in a minute. Please, see about the children."

The house was a mess. I tried not to focus on the damage and headed blindly for the basement.

When I got to the head of the stairs, I saw the first of several problems. The north kitchen wall had collapsed and most of it had landed directly in front of the Dutch door that led to the basement. Big as I was, I wasn't at all sure I could get through.

I was puzzling over my next move when Maggie came up behind me.

"Seth! Kathleen! Annie! Are you all right?"

There was a prayer in every word and a big one in my heart.

"Mom!"

"Seth, is that you? Is everyone okay?"

"I don't know. . . . Kathleen . . . Kathleen . . . Kathleen's okay, I'm okay, but I can't find Annie."

"She was in the basement with you, wasn't she?"

"Yes, but Kathleen and I put our heads down—like at school for drills—when we heard the noise, you know . . . and I . . . I'll look."

It took maybe forty-five eternal seconds before he called up again.

"Mom, she's here. She must have run toward the stairs and slipped or something. She . . . she's not awake."

If only we could get down there.

"Seth, listen to me. Are there any marks, a cut on her head, a bump, or anything bleeding?"

Forty-five more eternal seconds.

Kathleen answered this time. "I can't find anything. No bumps, just old bruises, you know, from falling off her bike and skates and stuff."

"Is she . . . she is breathing, though?"

"Yes."

"Can you get to the bathroom or is it blocked?"

"It's clear."

"Then get some cold water and a washcloth and try to wake her up. It's possible that with all the excitement she might have fainted."

More prayer.

I should have thought of it before, but I suddenly remembered the garage entrance to the basement. When I started to bolt for it, Maggie stopped me.

"It's no use that way, Judge. The brick side walls are down in front of the garage doors. We'd never get in that way. And we'll never get the car out either."

There was a kind of defeat in the way she said that.

If help didn't come to us we wouldn't be able to go for it. Maggie was having another pain, and I wasn't sure how much longer before they really got regular.

"She's waking, Mom! She seems okay."

A very small voice, quieter than normal, asked, "Do you get your ten hunnert for passing Go now?"

A victory! We needed that!

Maggie wouldn't, couldn't be really sure that they were all fine until she saw for herself. She tried once to move a few of the bricks, but she was afraid to do too much. Once the water broke, even if hard labor did not follow immediately, it could harm the baby.

There had to be a better way.

Maggie went for the phone in the pantry almost timidly . . . and, as might be expected, it was dead.

The question was, how long would it be that way? If it was a major cable, the phone company usually found the problem quickly and switched to some auxiliary. But if it was a local circuit, it could be days.

Another pain.

No, Maggie couldn't just sit and wait.

If no one came and the phones didn't work, then we were going to have to manage ourselves—first aid, digging out, a birth, whatever.

We would all do what we had to do.

Maggie and I studied every possible way of getting to the kids. We couldn't use any of the basement windows. They were either blocked or broken, and it was too dangerous to pull the children up or lower ourselves through them.

I walked to the road looking for signs that help was on the way. All I found was more debris and pieces of trees I didn't even recognize.

Seth's bunk beds were a quarter mile down the road, and half the south wall of his room was strewn in a circle around them.

So that put us right back at square one.

"What do the stairs look like, Seth?"

"There're a few bricks here and there, but

okay, I guess. There's a lot of plaster and bricks at the top, though."

"Seth, there is no other way, and I don't know how long it will be before someone comes. Do you think you and the girls can climb over the bricks?"

"I don't know, Mom. Some of those bricks look pretty loose. We wouldn't know what to hold onto."

There were several minutes where all either thought or prayed, and one or both systems worked because Seth had an idea.

"Mom, wait a minute. What about the bunk bed ladder? It has that extension cross bar at the top. Wouldn't that be wide enough to reach beyond the doorjamb on either side? Couldn't we hook it on and secure it with something? Then, even if the bricks slipped, we'd have something to hang onto."

I went off in search of the ladder, and Maggie kept reassuring the kids that the storm was over. I found it with the beds and bricks from Seth's room, and was relieved to see that it was in one piece.

It took precious minutes to drag the ladder back, but I had to take my time or risk splintering the wood.

Seth and Kathleen steadied the ladder at the bottom. Maggie and I positioned it at the top. Seth had been right. There was a three-inch extension of wood on either side of the door-jamb that held it in place. I pushed a few bricks to secure it still more and steadied it with my paws.

It was unanimous that Annie should go first.

Annie didn't cry even once. Maggie kept talking to her the whole time. When Annie got to the top, she held my paw and pulled herself up smiling.

Maggie squeezed her so tightly I thought she might break. Maggie checked her all over, every limb, her head, her neck, looking for bruises and punctures.

By some miracle, there were none.

Kathleen was next. She was a real trooper. She kept saying how easy it was, maybe to help Seth when it was his turn or maybe just to reassure herself. She put her arms around my neck and hugged me. "You big dumb hero, you got us where it was safe, didn't you?"

I don't think anyone saw me blush.

Maggie, with tears in her eyes, held Kathleen, too, for several minutes.

Seth started up then, and we felt close to winning. But he was heavier than the girls, and there was no one to steady the ladder from the bottom. When his extra twenty pounds hit the second rung, the ladder began to slip. . . .

It wasn't one terrific act. It was just an instant when I didn't know what to do. Seth,

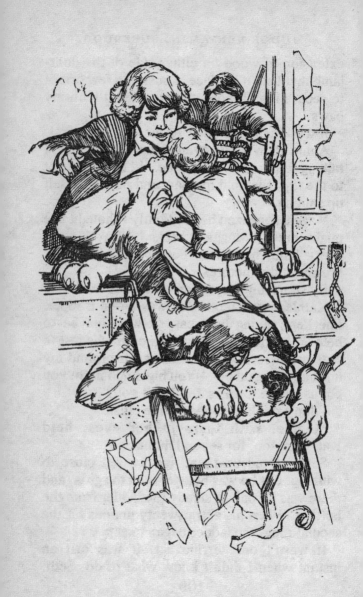

the young man I'd grown up with, would have fallen back down the debris-littered stairs if I had not lunged all my weight on the ladder.

Maggie and Annie and Kathleen grabbed paws and a tail and hung on.

And Seth, not for one second losing his cool, made it.

Over the ladder, over me, my tummy pressed to its limits against the bricks and bits of glass, and into the arms of his mother.

There were a few more tears and kisses then and, against my better judgment, I joined in.

For that moment, Seth and Kathleen and Annie were just glad to be in their mother's arms. But when another pain came, Maggie had to pull back. The children looked past their mother and saw the devastation that had been their home.

Annie looked like she might go into shock. Kathleen began to whimper, and Seth was fighting back the tears.

The house, the mess . . . it was scary. And there was more—the unspoken fear that un-nerved us all. Where was Tom?

Maggie tried the phone again, but she couldn't get a dial tone. She hung up and turned to survey the worst of it.

When you spend hours of love and laughter in a place, it seems to become a part of you. So

111

the broken mess we were looking at was like a little piece of each of us.

It looked like the kitchen had got the worst of it.

The lights were out, and the clock had stopped at two thirty-nine. I could still smell the stew. The Crock-Pot with its earthenware dish was sitting on the only part of the counter that appeared untouched. It would stay warm for hours, even with the power off.

It was strange to look at the spot where the refrigerator and cabinets had been and to see straight through to the patio. Even stranger— the sky was blue and warm, and the faintest edge of a rainbow was pointing east.

In Kathleen's bedroom and the living room, there wasn't a pillow out of place. But half of Seth's room had disappeared, and not a book remained on the library shelves.

I spotted Annie's teddy bear wedged under the dry sink in the dining room and brought it to her. When last she saw it, it had been standing guard over the Monopoly money, which was scattered everywhere. Annie cocked her head a bit and, seeing a long-lost friend, decided things were not all that bad.

Kathleen spoke honestly. "Oh, Mom, what are we going to do?"

"Well, Kathleen, we're going to cope."

Annie chimed in, "Oh, I'll have a Coke too."

Seth said that was a great idea except the refrigerator was nowhere around.

"What about Dad?"

I knew it would be Kathleen who finally asked what everyone else was thinking.

"Try the phone again, Kathleen."

"It's still dead."

"Seth, see if you can find one of our transistor radios and we'll listen to the news. Probably the tornado's path wouldn't be wide enough to catch both us and the business areas in the south and west. And anyway, Dad may still be in East St. Louis. I expect him to walk in very soon and ask 'What's for supper?' "

Maggie got another pain. It seemed to me they were only eight minutes apart by now. With the car in the garage behind a fallen brick wall, need I mention the state of my nerves?

Maggie sent the children to take a happy inventory. For every bad thing they found they had to look for two good things. If a wall was down, maybe they could find a picture that had survived, or a toy or a book. I went along to watch for danger spots.

Then, after fifteen minutes, Maggie called us together again.

"I don't think this baby is going to wait."

I had been afraid of that.

I knew Maggie would not for an instant have

113

chosen this time and this place to have a baby.
But isn't that the way it usually is?

Maggie was watching the children. Being
frank and honest with them was one thing, but
having to enlist their help at a time like this . . .
well, she would have given anything to have it
some other way.

Seth and Kathleen just looked at each other.
Annie started cheering. "Oh goodee, oh
goodee, our baby is going to be boring!"

Boring? *Boring?*

Not on your life.

But born.

Chapter 13

After thinking it through, Maggie decided to have the baby in the master bathroom. Even though the girls' rooms and the living room were still intact, she wasn't sure what the missing end walls had done to weaken the house's structure. She knew that small middle rooms were second in safety only to basements during storms.

We brought every blanket and towel we could find, and arranged pillows in the tub so Maggie could be comfortable.

Every few minutes, Seth and Kathleen would take turns trying the phone again.

The time between the pains got shorter.

If Maggie wasn't having an easy time of it

she was holding up well. The kids were very attentive. Kathleen combed Maggie's hair. Seth found some lemon drops for her. I wrestled playfully with Annie.

We said the rosary. Twice.

We sang songs.

We played Riddle Marie.

And, in between all these diversions, Maggie tried to explain to the children what to expect.

"You have to concentrate on the joy, kids, the wonder of a new life. And then the hurting doesn't seem so bad."

"Did it hurt when I was born?"

"How about me?"

"And *me!?*"

Yes. It always does, some. But it doesn't last very long. And when you hold that new life for the first time you forget the pain."

Kathleen, ever practical, finally said it. "But what do we *do*, Mom?"

"Well, for starters, you must remember not to be frightened. The baby won't be all clean and pretty right away, but a baby can still feel love. From that very first minute, the baby will know that we will take care of all its needs. Very, very gently, you will help guide the baby out of its little world into our big world. Then what has been the baby's home will follow the baby in birth through Mom. That's why I told you to bring all the towels."

If Seth was embarrassed, he didn't let on. He knew this was too important.

Kathleen's eyes were sparkling in happy anticipation of something she was to be a part of. She would offer more than moral support.

When Maggie sent Kathleen to help Annie find a music box to play for the coming O'Riley, I knew it was getting close. I was pacing like crazy. I couldn't stand by and do nothing.

Maggie must have read my mind.

"Seth, I think we should send Judge for help," Maggie said. "I really thought Tom would be home by now, but since he's not someone should know what's happening at the O'Rileys' today."

"I'll go, Mom," Seth answered.

"No, I've thought of that. But I will need you here. We have Annie to consider, and a new baby, and an extra pair of arms can't be spared."

"Mom, how's the Judge going to tell any-one?"

"We'll write a note and pin it to his collar. All the Judge has to do is pester someone till they read it."

Seth still looked skeptical.

"Seth, I'm a little afraid, too. It will help to know you're here and the Judge is out there, and you're both on my team."

117

Seth found some paper and a black magic marker. He printed in large bold letters:

*HEAVY DAMAGE AT
O'RILEY HOME
MOTHER IN LABOR
PLEASE SEND HELP*

Seth pinned the note to my choke collar with a large diaper pin. It was so obvious, it was bound to be noticed.

Kathleen and Annie came back then with the music box that played "Born Free."

A sign, I guess.

It put me in the mood for charging off.

Seth explained to Kathleen and Annie that *he* had decided to send me off to find help. Then he winked at his mom.

Before I left the house Maggie said once more, "Don't waste time, Judge. Head for Tom's office, but show the note to anyone!"

It was a big order, but I wasn't going to let Maggie down. It was twelve miles to Tom's office, but if I crossed Steven's Creek at the narrow north end I would pass the Shadow Lane subdivision. I figured I could persuade someone there to read the note.

I didn't slow down once. I kept seeing Maggie's face.

It had been a wet spring, and the creek was higher at the point of crossing than I remembered. Once I slipped on a rock and fell to my knees.

Drat. Wet fur. It wouldn't enhance my powers of persuasion.

I was running very fast and panting hard when I came to the edge of Shadow Lane. But when I saw it I stopped in shock.

Those beautiful homes had felt the tornado too. One whole block had nothing but foundations remaining. Cars were buried under roofing shingles, and trees and shrubs were uprooted and scattered. I could hear children crying and other dogs whimpering.

From somewhere a policeman was speaking calmly into a bullhorn. "All right, people, this is not a circus, please move on. We need this road cleared." He was trying to divert a line of cars driven by people who had come to see the damage. Every so often he would let someone through, probably someone with family in Shadow Lane.

I saw a man sitting on a boulder in front of a house that had lost only the garage. I tried to get his attention, nuzzling my nose on his hand, putting my head on his knee.

He patted my head once, but he didn't look up.

There were a lot of other people, but they all seemed preoccupied. They had troubles of their own.

My best bet was to try the policeman, even though I would have to weave through traffic to get to him.

I was running for the road when I looked down to avoid stepping on some glass.

The note was gone!

I could still feel the pin—Seth had been so careful to secure it—but the note was no longer attached. It must have gotten lost in the creek. How could I have been so foolish!

I was sick and at the point of despair when the most remarkable coincidence saved me.

In the line of cars by the policeman was Tom's yellow El Camino with Tom at the wheel. He must have been trying to get home. He had probably taken the northern route into Decatur from East St. Louis when he got caught in a traffic jam of gawking spectators.

I was so excited, I went charging blindly toward him.

If there had been confusion before, I certainly didn't help. A St. Bernard had no place in traffic, especially that kind of traffic.

Horns started honking like crazy. Not only did I pretend not to notice, but I imagined them as a rough arrangement of Annie's musical "Born Free" and it gave me courage. I knew I had to catch Tom's attention before he took off.

As big as I was, the cars were bigger, and there were only two cars between Tom and the turnoff to MacArthur Road. If I missed him now I would never catch him.

The policeman's whistle had joined the honks. Everyone seemed to notice me *except* Tom.

Then I saw my chance.

The traffic was moving so slowly that a pretty teenager driving a red Mustang next to Tom's turned off her engine to put on some lipstick and comb her hair. She was talking to her friends in the front seat and hadn't noticed that a St. Bernard was following her.

I took a flying leap, first onto the trunk of the red Mustang, and then onto its roof.

The policeman was really whistling now. I didn't know what kind of ticket he could give me—reckless Mustang-hopping?—but, finally, Tom looked up. I could see him mouth the words, *"Judge Benjamin!!!!!!?"*

The teenager had perhaps wondered about

the thud on her roof, but that was all. She had finished primping and began easing on down the street.

All I could do was hang on. It was cowardly, I know, but at that point I closed my eyes. I remembered a page in my past with the Gremlin, and I didn't think I could survive that kind of craziness twice.

But the policeman's whistle got louder, and the girl stopped the car. Tom came running up, and I slid off just as he got there.

"Big fella, what are you doing here?" He started to pat me and saw the diaper pin on my collar. Tom frowned. Then he noticed a small jagged corner of paper matted in the deep fur on my neck—it was so small I'd missed it. It was all that was left of the important note, and it was smudged:

IN LABOR

YELP

The policeman, furious, was running up to us. Tom went for the heavy offense. "Sir, my family, my wife's in labor. I'll need an ambulance."

The policeman was still looking at me strangely. "Where do you live?"

"North Bearsdale Road. I've been out of town till now."

The policeman sighed helplessly. "No ambulance can get through. Highway 121 caught tornado debris for miles!"

"Then a doctor. . . ."

"All staff doctors report to the hospital in this emergency."

"I've got to help her!" Tom pleaded.

"I'll radio in the problem, but try to get her to the hospital yourself. Make a wide western circle. Orchard Road is west enough to have missed most of the tornado, I think. It will be the fastest way. It would take an ambulance over an hour just to get this far."

Tom and I raced to the El Camino in four giant steps. He opened the hatch for me to hop in back. The policeman cleared cars out of our way and waved us off with crossed fingers.

I guessed I wasn't under arrest.

Tom tried to speed, but branches and debris littered the road. Several times we had to stop completely and pull some big ones off our path. We were taking too long, and we both knew it. If it took this much time to get to Maggie, how much longer before we could get her to the hospital? That's when Tom thought of Dr. Steinberg, the retired obstetrician who lived in the remodeled farmhouse west of the fair-grounds.

"Of course," Tom said out loud, snapping his fingers. "Dr. Steinberg! We have to practically go by his house with this western path anyway!"

Chapter 14

Finally, we got where we wanted to go.

We pulled into Dr. Steinberg's drive, and panic set in. The drive now ended where the garage used to be. All that was left was a lawn mower and one untouched wall with a neat pegboard and properly placed tools. Tom stared for a minute, hoping the slam of his car door wouldn't cause the wall to fall.

Then he saw Dr. Steinberg coming around the side of the house. Tom knew it wasn't the time or place to laugh, but he was having a hard time holding back.

Dr. Steinberg, six feet tall, gray-haired, and over eighty if he was a day, had one lens of his glasses missing. He was wearing jeans, suspenders, a navy blue T-shirt, and perfectly polished wingtip shoes. And he was taking out the garbage. Except, from the looks of things, he hadn't been able to locate the garbage cans.

This was going to be Maggie's savior?

The doctor smiled when he finally saw us. He spoke as if he'd known us for years.

"Danged if I can find it. Did you pass a can on your way up? Just bought two new ones last month, too."

Tom wasn't up to being social. "Doc, I need your help. I think my wife is in trouble, and I can't get an ambulance in or a doctor out to help her."

"Oh?"

"The tornado. All the doctors are reporting to the hospital and the roads aren't passable, and she started labor."

"Hey, fella, wait a minute. I haven't delivered a baby in eighteen years!!"

"Sir, you're the best I can do."

Dr. Steinberg started to laugh, a big hearty laugh. The honesty of that remark really caught him. Suddenly they were both laughing, and we knew he would go.

Doc handed him the garbage. "I'll get my bag."

Tom stood there holding the garbage, trying to figure out just exactly what to do with it.

When Doc came hurrying out of his house, Tom threw it in the back of the El Camino with me.

Not my favorite kind of traveling companion. I mean, there must have been a week's worth of garbage, judging by its fragrance.

"You left out a few details," Doc was saying.

"Tom. Tom O'Riley. And this is Judge Benjamin."

"Big thing, isn't he?" Dr. Steinberg said as he patted my head. Then, "If an ambulance can't get through, what makes you think we can make it?"

Tom hadn't completely thought this out, but he knew we had to try. "Well, we made it this far. Are you into jogging?"

"I'm afraid not."

"We'll have to go as far as we can in the car and then walk."

"If labor is already started . . . How many children do you have?"

"This will be four."

"Then we'd better make tracks. They don't fool around after number three."

Tom looked sick.

And he wasn't the only one.

We had to keep circling back when we ran into blocked roads, but we finally made it to the fairgrounds before driving became impossible.

That still left four miles.

We got out of the car and stared at each other. I was for running, but I knew the doc wouldn't get very far very fast.

Then Tom remembered the storage shed on the fairgrounds. Luckily, it was still standing. Those stupid minibikes that made so much noise all summer were stored there. Tom ran for it, Dr. Steinberg puffing behind him.

Locked.

And locked tight.

I gave it some good whacks with my paw but it wouldn't budge.

We'd need a crowbar to handle it. The nearest available crowbar might as well have been in Africa.

Dr. Steinberg sized up the situation. "I think I can handle this."

He opened his little black bag, took out a pick, and poked it into the keyhole.

Tom couldn't believe it.

Neither could I.

"After my wife died, I had all kinds of trouble remembering things, and I must have locked myself out of the house at least once a day. So I bought—"

Tom didn't wait for the rest of the explanation. The door opened and he bounded in, grabbing the two closest bikes.

I never thought I'd be glad to see those noisemakers.

Dr. Steinberg was taken aback.

"You've got to be kidding. Locks I know, but these?"

"Doc, we gotta try. Please!!!"

The nice thing about Dr. Steinberg was that, at eighty, he hadn't lost his sense of adventure.

"Oh, heck, what have I got to lose?"

Tom showed Doc how to get his going. "The switch at the bottom is gas. Turn the motor to run and squeeze the gear on the handle."

I recognized the familiar sound.

I led the way, uneasily aware that though Tom was right behind me, Dr. Steinberg wasn't exactly right behind him.

I glanced over my shoulder and saw the doc's confusion. The large man plunked himself on the tiny seat, got his balance, and took off, only to have to turn around to pick up his black bag. This proved more than a little problem, since he was sure he would need both hands for driving or hiding his eyes, whichever. He finally solved it by attaching the bag to his suspenders. This complicated things further, since the suspenders were then too weighted down to hold up his pants.

But off he went.

It was a rough few miles.

I was way ahead. I stood at the top of our hill, barking for all I was worth to encourage speed. I saw the top of Tom's head bouncing up the hill and our good doc a hundred feet behind.

I was aware of the somewhat less than miraculous rescue two men on minibikes represented. Well, beggars can't be choosers.

The big doc went through a ditch—he seemed to be having trouble because of that black bag, which kept springing up from his suspenders. Oh, heavens!—they finally popped altogether.

I retrieved the bag, which I figured was essential, and left the suspenders for a more opportune time. When Doc finally got off the mini-bike, I realized that they were pretty essential too, as his pants kept sliding down past modesty.

Tom was halfway to the house, his speed not so great as to miss the damage before him. Crumbled walls, the bunk beds on end. . . . I knew what he must be thinking.

I charged ahead, showing him the quickest, safest route.

He parked the bike in what had been the kitchen, and followed me to the family.

We were just inside the room when we heard it. It was the cry of a newborn baby.

Seth was supporting his mother by the shoulders as she struggled to tie the umbilical cord. Kathleen—dear, sweet, efficient Kathleen—was holding a perfectly beautiful baby girl in warm dry towels. Annie Elizabeth was winding up the music box and singing for all she was worth.

None of us will ever forget that moment.

All the devastation, all the fear of that strange day seemed never to have happened. It was washed clean in that miracle.

Maggie looked up, weary but smiling. "Tough day at the office, dear?"

Dr. Steinberg, several steps behind the action, came in huffing. "Now, which of you ladies is expecting?"

When that met with giggles, he turned to Seth and decided to greet him with his old navy salute.

Except his right hand had heretofore been holding up his pants.

Ooooops.

I made tracks to find those suspenders.

It had been the single most destructive onslaught of tornadoes in almost fifty years—April 3 and April 4, 1974. They struck in eleven midwestern and southern states. Total damages were about $700 million, with three hundred fifty deaths and more than four thousand injuries.

We had been lucky. Very lucky.

For us there had not been death, but birth.

Three weeks later, on April 24, 1974, when the pickup, cleanup, buildup was in full swing, we christened Maura Louise.

The party at the house after the ceremony was one to be remembered forever.

Father James was there, and Father Leo from the parish, who brought his sisters. Father Herbert, Maggie's priest from grade school, also came. Sister Mary was there, and Sister Joseph and Sister Teresa, Kathleen and Seth's teachers. Dr. Lacey came, and Dr. Steinberg. Dr. Steinberg bought red socks to match his favorite red suspenders especially for the occasion. He had the lens in his glasses fixed too. The Lockleys came, and Grammy and Pa drove all those miles to celebrate the christening. Some Connecticut family made it, and great-grandma from Chicago, and aunts and uncles and cousins galore.

Henry was there, of course. He was not at all impressed by the crowds and spent most of the day pouting behind the velvet couch. He perked up some once, when Annie found him and played a game of catch with that silly orange ball.

Tom had fashioned a long picnic table from

134

the boards and debris that had littered the yard. Since the house was a long way from being repaired and the sun was shining, the feasting was outdoors.

There was cold rare roast beef and potato salad and molded aspic and sweet baked beans and mashed potatoes with a cheddar cheese topping and butterscotch pies and French silk pies and garden vegetables and champagne and strawberry fizz.

Maggie swore she would put me on a grapefruit diet. But I didn't care.

It was a celebration of life. I was just so grateful to be there.

Imagine, another O'Riley to love.

Welcome, Maura.

9

ABOUT THE AUTHOR

JUDITH WHITELOCK McINERNEY grew up in the small town of Metropolis, Illinois, and started her writing career at age seven with the printing of her Brownie Troop minutes in the *Metropolis News*. Eventually she wrote her own column during high school, and went on to graduate from the College of Journalism at Marquette University in Michigan. After marrying her college sweetheart, she had four children, who figure in this first novel with their own lovable St. Bernard, Judge Benjamin, as the hero. Her children, three girls and a boy, range in age from kindergarten through high school and are sure to be part of the author's upcoming books. The McInerneys presently make their home in Decatur, Illinois.

ABOUT THE ILLUSTRATOR

During his teen years, LESLIE MORRILL worked in a zoo, which sparked his interest in animal stories such as *Judge Benjamin: Superdog*. He developed his artistic talents at the Graduate School of the Museum of Fine Arts at Boston and the Cranbrook Academy in Michigan. After working as an assistant professor in a Pennsylvania college, he returned to Boston as a commercial artist and to illustrate books. Since then he has over 60 books to his credit and is currently writing his own picture book.